“The Egyptian Connection”

to

The Lost Civilization

Egyptian Connection
To The Lost Civilization

ISBN Number: 979-8-9903350-4-2

Printed in the United States of America

“The Egyptian Connection”

to

The Lost Civilization

by
K.J.Goss

Prologue

"I heard you mumble something about Egypt the other day," Dan mentioned in passing, but not being serious.

His words were directed at Violet, (aka) Dove of Spring.

Dan, Eric and Violet were relaxing under the stars enjoying their Cognac at Violet's house, now Violet's and Eric's house.

Violet was taken by surprise by his remarks as was Eric. Eric, looked at Violet with questioning eyes.

"I didn't think anybody heard me," she replied. "It was just a passing thought," answered Violet calmly. "After all we just went through it triggered a thought about China and Egypt."

"You're not really serious, are you?" quizzed Eric.

"No my love, as I said it was just a passing thought. Both China and Egypt seemed so enmeshed in the Lost Civilization, I just wondered if they also had their own Disney world advertisements as I mentioned the other day."

Eric smiled now and relaxed.

"It stands to reason that they both would and who knows there may be others. We know that China traded with Italy if that's what it was called way back then."

Smiling herself now Dove of Spring remarked,

"See, I'm not the only crazy one here. You thought along the same lines."

Dan, being his usual self commented,

"I thought the both of you were crazy and now you're driving me crazy."

Chapter 1

Their last view of the scenes of the Lost Civilization still weighing heavily on their minds the three jungle weary friends finally arrived home. Dan politely excused himself heading for his own house and some much needed rest.

Eric and Violet settled themselves into the cushiony welcoming reclining chairs in the living room, both showing the obvious weariness of their two months in the jungle. They sighed heavily as they both kicked their boots off.

Weary but happy for their accomplishments, neither could say what satisfied them most: the physical finds in the jungle or the ultimate discovery of the Lost Civilization, both in the Yucatan and here at home.

Finally able to relax uninterrupted they both silently smiled their love for one another.

Silence prevailed for quite a spell each lost in their own thoughts.

Dove of Spring was extremely proud of her Navaho Heritage, yet this new connection to the Golden Lady, and her actual possibility of going further back to a connection to Nefertiti and Egypt kept her thoughts in constant motion. She, herself could not distinguish between curiosity and pride. Perhaps it was both. Actually, down deep inside she felt the Egyptian connection to Nefertiti was real. Why else would she be experiencing these strange unexplained feelings. Her mind was in constant turmoil since these discoveries, yet she was now happy in her new world of marriage and living in the present.

Shyly she admitted to herself that she missed and longed for the council of Whispering Wind.

On the other side of the room equally disturbing thoughts were spinning through Eric's mind also longing for the King's riddling council.

Some twenty minutes passed by quickly with both Dove of Spring and Hunter of Stories lost in their own private worlds.

Quietly, almost in a whisper, Violet spoke.

"**C**an we go back to the Lost World. I really would like to."

Not totally surprised by her comment, Eric answered quickly.

"**I** think I would like that myself." Here Eric paused, then added, "But perhaps not today. We can head out first thing in the morning. It will be dark by the time we got there."

Violet looked very disappointed.

"**I** always knew you were a Party Pooper" she returned with a smile. "Just for that you can fix dinner tonight while I go and take a shower."

"**W**hy? Is dinner broken ?" he quipped.

Not waiting for any further reply she stood and headed for the bathroom.

"**I** guess I know who's boss around here," he yelled after her.

Chapter 2

A little after sunrise Dove of Spring was nudging Eric awake.

"Are you going to sleep the whole day away?" she chided.

"I didn't hear the monkeys howl yet," he answered in a sleepy mumble.

On a more serious side Violet continued, "Come on sleepy head we have a long day ahead of us."

It was then Eric remembered the promised return to the Lost World.

A decent breakfast and the pair were on their way.

"Perhaps we should call Dan," suggested Eric.

"No need my love. Remember he had his teens and class work today," answered Violet positively. She also remembered some snacks and lemon drink. The lemon drink was the remembrance of Whispering Wind. Set and ready they headed for the four corners area at the far end of the reservation. An approximately two hour drive.

It was an uneventful yet not boring ride. The pair still marveled at the beauty of the early sun on its treasures of sand and rock. Even though they had viewed it countless times, the ever changing color was always captivating.

Their destination reached, Violet had the excitement of a child at Christmas.

"Slow down love, I don't think it is going anyplace.

Not after thousands of years."

Her cheeks flushed as she smiled.

Entering the old structure they went straight for the now not so hidden door.

"Remind me to get together with Dan and make this disappear again," Eric said aloud.

"Disappear, yes, but not completely," offered Violet.

Eric nodded in agreement.

Eric turned and pulled the handle and the old door creaked open. The darkness of the steps stared back at the couple. They descended the first few steps and as before a subdued light again showed the steep decent. Even though Eric had witnessed this miracle many times before he still marveled at this ancient yet advanced technology.

Violet remained silent though her heart and mind were bathed in wonderment. Eric again removed his boots and placed them appropriately in the doorway to assure they would not be locked in.

Hand in hand Dove of Spring and Hunter of Stories entered the blackness of this antique world and as before, the night dissipated into the forever blue which gave way to the real rainbow of the colors in the natural environment. Various shades of green outlined the fields and mountains, while the crimson and yellow intertwined to highlight the natural beauty of this world. A beauty which is too often overlooked or taken for granted.

Violet was frozen in place for many minutes, again totally captivated by the scene before her. She felt a peace come over her like never before. Eric left her undisturbed for he was experiencing the very same thing.

"How is this possible and why is this here and in the Yucatan? They are both the most unlikely of places. Perhaps that is the answer."

These thoughts played on his mind for quite a while.

Dove of Spring, at last brought her mind into focus and stepped forward to again follow the path of beauty. Unlike the first introduction to this miracle of technology, she moved slowly along the path mentally digesting every nuance of beauty. Every thing she viewed was perfection. At least in her mind. Even though her extensive engineering background allowed her much understanding of the world, this miracle before her was truly and totally baffling.

Eric, though many feet behind Violet was also puzzled with the same thoughts.

"Now is when I wish I could connect with the king again. He offered many answers through his riddles but never a total explanation of the Lost Civilization."

A thought of being part of this unexpected world materialized to both as if planted by an outside force.

Wandering off the walking path, each entered an area of grass and trees, to touch, smell and become one with. Violet was deeply immersed into nature itself while Eric had his mind spinning as to the how and why of it. Time stood still here even though the hands on the clock were still spinning. They each continued at their own pace following this path of peace and sublime beauty. Neither spoke a word not wanting to disturb the perfection of this Lost World.

Almost two hours slipped by and they found themselves at the path's beginning. Words were still not spoken as they methodically secured the door and climbed the steps to reality still in total silence.

Once back at the car Violet retrieved the snacks and lemon drink. This was also shared in silence as each observed the desert surroundings. The whole world appeared to be at peace now.

Ever so slowly the present world reasserted itself into the mind and body of the loving couple.

"Let's go out for dinner. I truly don't feel like cooking tonight," offered Dove of Spring with her "You can't refuse me" smile.

Slightly taken aback by her statement Eric dared not refuse.

"Just the two of us," he posed.

Violet's eyes glowed more than usual.

Back at the house Violet disappeared into the bedroom before Eric even had time to close the door.

Ten minutes later she reappeared dressed exactly as their first dinner date. Buckskin dress and boots along with her raven black hair reminding Eric of that first actual date. Her appearance was enough to turn any man's head.

"Well, come on slow poke, dinner awaits," she voiced with a smile. "Get changed out of those dusty clothes."

He kissed her cheek, "Yes Mama," and headed for the shower.

A short drive found them at their favorite steak house. Dinner along with the right wine sealed a perfect day. Returning to the house they retired to the back yard to enjoy the moon and another glass of wine.

A long silence was interrupted by Dove of Spring.

"Let's go to Egypt."

Eric, almost dropping his wine, spilling some on his shirt, questioned, "Are you serious. We just returned from Central America. Why do you want to go to Egypt?"

"There are a few reasons actually," she smiled coyly. "Perhaps there is another hidden Lost Civilization there."

"We can't just go digging tunnels in another country," Eric put forth confused by her statement.

Violet then exposed her true reasons. Smiling, yet serious she explained her true feelings.

"Now that I truly know who I am, I would like to further study my heritage. What better way to do it than go to the source. Your Golden Lady has shown the way and I would like to complete her quest."

Eric remained silent just staring at his beloved,

knowing deep inside what she was longing for. The final truth of her namesake. She deserved to know the answers to the unasked questions. Is she really a direct descendant of "The beautiful one is come". Deep inside they both believed this to be true. Further research would be the final truth. Eric knew he would want the same clarification if he were subject to that possibility.

He remained silent for a while in a confusion of thought.

"Do you realize how expensive a trip like that would be?" he put forth, not even convinced himself of the argument against.

"I have not been idle just here on the reservation. As an engineer I have been able to put aside some money for a rainy day and right now it is raining," she answered with her ever captivating smile.

Smiling now, almost laughing, Eric shared his own thoughts.

"I have spent so much time in the jungle I haven't been spending anything. I believe it is raining on me also. I have some savings and I won't let you go alone. So my love, Egypt it is but let us study and prepare first."

"Party Pooper," Violet answered even though her own thoughts were the same.

The next three weeks were planing, research and study on anything Egyptian.

Arrangements had been made through Carlos for hotel reservations near the great pyramids. The possibility of a guide or historical contact were also secured by Carlos. Dan was of course asked to join them but to him his first responsibility was his class.

The next two weeks they worked diligently in researching whatever they could gather. After a few days of endless reading they gained nothing they were not already familiar with. It was almost disappointing.

To break the monotony Dove of Spring decided they

should have a break As a change of pace they returned to the hogan of Whispering Wind, which, of course, was now an historical museum. There were still two unopened boxes to sort through. They were well hidden in one of the many underground storage areas Whispering Wind was so cleaver at concealing. The first box was again many papers outlining world wide trade agreements with no identifiable dates but obviously ancient.

Almost not wanting to bother with the second box yet deciding to since it was the last of it, Violet set about opening it. This particular box was well sealed compared to the rest of the others. Finding a claw hammer and strong screwdriver she at last managed the top. Here she froze in place. Eric, at the time was off elsewhere. She was viewing books and papers and all things Egyptian.

*"**H**e must have known all along. That explains him in possession of the picture of the Golden Lady."*

She remained steadfastly staring at the books. At last finding the courage she reached for the top book, hesitating slightly but finally opening it. As she thumbed through it she saw it was obviously outlining the history and life and reign of Akhenaton. *"Who was Akhenaton ?"* she asked herself.

Flipping through the pages the name Nefettiti caught her attention. She paused here and read a few paragraphs. She was the wife of Akhenaton. *His original name was* Amenophis IV. Violet realized more reading would be necessary to understand more but this moment was not the time. She skimmed through the rest of the book picking up the name Nefertiti here and there.

"**I** know Eric will want to read this also," she said aloud.

The other books were also facts of Egypt spanning many centuries. She realized this would be required reading but again not at this moment. She remained with the books in her lap staring ahead at absolutely nothing, her minds eye seeing only the "Golden Lady"realizing she was truly a descendent and part of the history of Egypt, though a very distant part.

Eric returned to find Violet exactly where he left her.

She acted as if frozen in place. He called her name softly so as not to startle her. There was no reply. He tried again and still no reply. On a whim his third try was different.

"My "Golden Lady" are you receiving an audience."

"Yes, but only if----"

Here she hesitated and turned to look at Eric smiling. As if suddenly awakening she flushed crimson.

"Eric, I'm so sorry. Please forgive me. I don't know what I was thinking."

"Yes you do and so do I, my queen. Welcome back to my world."

"I feel so foolish."

Still flushed she turned away.

"Perhaps we should forget Egypt."

"Not on your life my queen. You have every right to know your history now that you know the truth."

Violet, still facing away, remained silent for a few moments. Finally turning to Eric she questioned; "What's wrong with me? Why am I acting this way? I'm frightened my love."

Hunter of Stories moved to her, enfolding her in his arms.

"No need to be frightened sweetheart, I'm here and always will be. We are in this new world together," he whispered comfortingly. They both were hushed in the moment, their thoughts flying aimlessly.

Eric ended their mutual pause voicing his thoughts out loud.

"Most of my life I never put much stock in what they call the Paranormal. That is, until I met the King and soon after, Whispering Wind. This gave me a whole new outlook of certain things. Right now my love I believe you are experiencing the very same thing. Ten years ago I would not have believed what we are both under going at this time. Please consider my thoughts. This is real and now and obviously beyond our control. So to answer your question, there is nothing wrong with you."

Slowly she turned in his arms, smiled and kissed him.

"Thank you," Laughing now she followed with, "Okay, so we are both crazy. I think I like it that way."

"**W**ithout the King and Whispering Wind I guess we are on our own. Together my Dove, I believe we can do it. Now show me what books you are hiding in your lap."

Violet returned to reality feeling totally renewed.

"**O**h, I almost forgot. These are all books of Egypt or in particular mentioning Nefertiti. It appears Whispering Wind knew all along but chose to keep it a secret."

"**U**ntil the right time." added Eric. "Let's face it, this Lost Civilization has got us all in quite a quandary. Why only now is it coming to light? More importantly why only us and my Maya friends?"

Violet, sort of back to normal, now responded confidently, "To me, the answer to that inquiry would be because you and your Maya scientist friends awakened your King, and in you, he recognized a Chosen One to continue his work of teaching about his Lost Civilization."

Equally comfortable now Eric responded; "And let us not forget you becoming the "Golden Lady" and the sudden pressure put on you. We have both been under the strain of notoriety, which neither of us asked for or wanted, yet it seems with this Lost Civilization we have both accepted this almost unwanted challenge."

At this point Violet looked at Eric directly and smiling whispered;

"**Y**ou are absolutely correct my "Chosen One."

Smiling in return Eric replied.

"**I** accept that title coming from you my "Golden Lady and Queen."

They laughed lightly and hugged each other both feeling better about their life ahead.

Now having resigned themselves to natures fate and decisions they went about their days activities with a happy and confident note.

Gathering as many books and journals as they could

from various libraries and book stores available, the next few weeks were devoted to research. Eric on Egypt in general and all he could gather in possible trade contracts. Dove of Spring concentrated on her historical namesake, Nefertiti.

Facts about this Egyptian Queen were sparse, at least in the books at their disposal. Perhaps, she hoped, their would be more background once they arrived in Egypt. A local historical library would fit the bill nicely.

Eric, in the meantime was having slightly better success. He came across bits and pieces of information regarding Trade and navigational trade routes. One article that drew his immediate interest was the finding by underwater Archeologists of a sunken Egyptian vessel off the coast of what is now the Carolinas. He would follow up on this bit of information the best he could.

The next few weeks were busy with rather boring research. The only lighter mood parts of the day were periodic visits from Dan, ever the clown. Repeated trips to the hogan, now the museum, of Whispering Wind. This was history unto itself and deeper and older than most people would have figured.

A comfortable evening after dinner and a tiring day of research, Eric and Violet were enjoying a glass of wine outside at their three tree jungle. Violet who had been staring at the almost full moon broke the silence with a soft voice.

"**E**ric, I know this is going to sound crazy but I just had a really enlightening thought of the lost world beauty here on the reservation land and perhaps even the one in the Yucatan."

Here she hesitated not even sure herself of her own thoughts.

"**W**hat if ?" She paused again acting almost shy. "What if there is more to see than what little we saw. We stayed to the main pathway so to speak. What about straying from that path? Is there any more? If these people constructed the ideal world, why keep it so limited?"

Eric, slowly smiling and looking directly at Violet replied, also softly;

"**N**ow who sounds like the "Chosen One".

He let that register for a few seconds, then followed with,

"You may be correct in your assessment. Similar thoughts have crossed my mind."

With a broad full smile Violet replied;

"First thing tomorrow then? I'll go and refill our wine."

Watching her walk to the house Eric laughed to himself.

"I don't know which one of us is worse."

~ ~ ~ ~ ~ ~

As agreed without it being vocalized Dove of Spring and Hunter of Stories were up early having breakfast and preparing snacks for the day. By eight o'clock they were on their way. The route was becoming familiar now. Silence seemed to rule their ride, each absorbed in their own world of thought.

The now familiar darkness of the steps greeted them. Silence still reigned as they entered the world of ever blue sky. Only now did they act like children seeing the Lost World for the first time. Violet's smile was actually childlike. They silently went in different directions.

Walking some fifty yards or so Violet was suddenly taken by the beauty of certain flowers. Leaving the pathway she approached what caught her attention only to be even more surprised. Low and behind the floral display was a marble like stone standing on the perfectly trimmed grass. Much to her wonderment, but not really, she was staring at an obvious Egyptian cartouch. She could not actually read it but instinctively knew it referring to her namesake Nefertity. She felt that familiar tingle as with the Golden Lady.

"So this is real," she thought to herself. "It must be real. I'm living it right now in real time. How can this be?" she wondered. "Back in time but living it right now."

She longed for the wisdom of Whispering Wind and wondering why had he held this secret for so long.

Suddenly she was beginning to understand the secret of the Chosen Ones.

Most people of today are obsessed with the here and now. History has all been almost forgotten. Living for today was of the utmost importance.

But why? She pondered.

Obviously we are not as advanced as we believe we are. Especially after observing what I am right now. The difficulty of the Chosen Ones must have truly been overwhelming. No one would listen to one preaching of true peace and harmony.

"I think I now truly believe the mental anguish Eric has been going through. Having this responsibility thrust upon him, so to speak, I'm sure was an awesome mental challenge. I understand more now that I am similarly challenged with my connection with the Golden Lady and onto Nefertiti. The weight of this responsibility could be overwhelming, if we let it," she cautioned herself.

"Come back to reality Violet," she gently scolded.

"Continue what you came here to do."

She did gaze around at other things of beauty but her eyes continued to come back to the cartouch as if some power was drawing her there.

"Move on," she scolded again. Move on she did only to find a setting of mini Pyramids. The three great pyramids of Egypt laid out perfectly to the mathematical scale of the constellation of Orion, both distance and orientation wise, the tallest being only about fourteen inches high. They were beautifully arranged in a bed of unnameable flowers which cast ever moving shadows of color. As was all else in this "Lost Civilization," this was perfection

"This absolutely proves there was contact eons ago. No matter what today's professionals preach as doctrine. I wonder how and why we as a people became so short sighted."

She wished Eric was here to witness this and even photograph this impossible sight.

Violet no sooner finished this thought when she felt Eric's loving touch on her shoulder.

"I hope I didn't startle you, but I heard you talking to nothing.:

"This certainly is not nothing. Look here," as she pointed. Our Egyptian connection. Who knows how long there has been contact."

"Obviously long before today's beliefs," Eric replied.

Dove of Spring then proceeded to tell Eric about the cartouch. He could hear the happy enthusiasm in her voice, and he was happy for her.

"Who knows what other secrets are buried here in this wonder world?"

"What about you Eric. Did you discover anything we overlooked the last visit."

"Indeed I did love. More than I expected."

Violet's eyes sparkled even more at hearing these words.

"Well! Tell me, don't keep me hanging."

"Tell you what?" returned Eric.

With that answer Violet swatted his arm.

"Here we go with the spousal abuse again," he laughed.

"Keep up that attitude and next time I'll scalp you. Remember, I am part Navajo."

"Ah! But then you would have no to pick on," replied Eric with a big smile.

"Come with me and I'll show you."

Hand in hand they retraced Eric's path a good distance from where Violet was. Entering a hardly seen area reminded Violet of their Yucatan jungle home. At first she eyed nothing but trees, then suddenly spotted what Eric was excited about. Before them, well hidden, was a mini version of the King's tomb. There was no mistake about it. Every detail was duplicated including the hidden opening mechanism.

"This just further solidifies the fact that there was contact thousands of years ago," Violet stated firmly, more as if convincing herself than anyone else.

Eric joined with his own personal thoughts.

"True, but how do we go about convincing the world, especially with the strongly accepted paradigm that we face. We and our four Maya friends are facing a world of doubters of what we have been witness to over the last few months. I would also have doubted five years ago."

"What else is hidden in this wondrous place?" questioned an excited Violet.

"It's not too late yet. Let's keep looking," she added.

Eric knew that as excited as she was there would be no deterring her from a continuous search.

They again went their separate ways with Violet returning to her Egypt find and continuing on from there.

Dove of Spring did not have to go too far. She was again surprised by a hidden stelae. This one was showing definite Chinese characters. The reverse side showed what appeared to be the west coast of North America. Bearing the marks of a navigation route headed South. Every now and then there was a mark inland, obviously a landing. Another impossibility as stated by some of our experts.

She decided then that she would have to get her own camera just for moments like this. It would undoubtedly save return trips to document these finds which would also help poor Eric not to have to work so hard to please everyone.

She moved on trying not to miss one turned over blade of grass. Here again she spotted something she almost stepped on. It was stone or marble about nine inches high. It reminded her of the Washington monument. It was the exact same shape. It was well planted in the ground and would not move, though she admittedly did not try to hard. It belongs here she told herself.

Down on hands and knees she viewed it closely. There were definite markings on all four sides. A writing of sorts she assumed, totally indecipherable to her.

"Eric must see this," she reminded herself. She drifted on finding nothing new.

"Perhaps another search at another time," she thought.

From there on her thoughts returned to Eric. Leaving

the past she went in search of him. She circled this whole "Lost World" finally seeing him waiting by the entranceway. He smiled and acknowledged her but uttered not a word. Stepping aside he indicated she leave first. He secured the entranceway and they made their way to the steps. Still not a word from either.

The snacks and lemon drink were welcomed by both but silence prevailed. Dove of Spring had seen Eric like this before and knew not to push. She was certain he would enlighten her in his own time.

The drive back to home remained silent. Once home Eric appeared normal again but his silent trip was not discussed. Violet did not push. He always gave her freedom of thought she could do at least so in kind.

They cooked outside, enjoying a light wine and watching the stars and spoke of the constellations.

Eric remarked, no matter what era of time you spoke of all were fascinated by the constellations and the heavenly movements.

Why? There never was an answer.

Chapter 3

"Did you enjoy your discoveries today ?"

"Frankly I did not think there would be anything new."

"I also was amazed that there was anything. Amazed and astounded. Particularly by the Egyptian and Chinese connections. Connections the world does not want to accept."

"My Dove of Spring, I owe you an apology for my behavior and stubbornness about returning here."

"There is no need my love. We are here and I accept your behavior. I know you must have your reasons. I shall not pry."

"Thank you for your understanding but I do wish to share with you my find. It was not a visible or tangible thing , It was more mind shattering than that."

Violet's interest was now more than peaked.

"Go on," she encouraged.

I really don't know how to explain. It truly was not a thing to describe. I guess you would call it a fleeting thought."

Confused but curious, Violet remained silent, giving Eric his time.

He appeared speechless again as if mind searching. At last, looking directly at Violet; "It was as if a voice was in my mind. Not like Atl or Whispering Wind," he paused, "More like a thought, I guess. A thought that was planted there by an outside power. I had no control over what was being placed in my mind."

"Was it good or bad?" Violet pursued.

"I can't say it was bad yet it was something I did not want to hear."

His words seemed to linger here as if the thought disturbed him. He finally came out with it.

"It recognized me as a "Chosen One". At first it was frightening but almost instantly became comforting. I don't really agree or want such recognition yet some how I feel that I have now accepted the challenge totally unconsciously. I had never been there before but there was a recognition by the "Lost World". I am to continue the work of Atl and Whispering Wind."

"Do you want to do that?" Violet asked quietly willing to accept whatever answer he gave.

"In all fairness to both Atl and Whispering Wind and of course that woman, "The Keeper of the Past", I accept this most onerous challenge. Let's face it though it will be like walking up a down escalator."

Violet was now all smiles and rushed to give Eric a warm embrace.

"I will always be at your side. Together we will accomplish anything, to quote your words. If we can't convince the world will you still be my Chosen One ?"

"Next stop Egypt," said a very enthusiastic and smiling Violet.

Eric dared not argue with her this time. He knew that she had to have final answers to her heritage.

"Why not?" he thought. *"I've never been to Egypt. It will be nice to compare their paradise with the Yucatan.*

Chapter 4

We had the usual boring, uninteresting flight that seemed to take forever. Arizona to Chicago to Atlanta to New York, to London and finally Egypt. We felt we had aged three years during the flight. We did, however, catch up on some of our Egyptian reading making many notes. Thank goodness we were in first class otherwise there would not have been enough room for anything.

As promised by Carlos there was a gentleman there to meet us and happily escorted us to our hotel. He then volunteered to be our guide if we found it necessary. I, without hesitation, accepted. At least until we found our bearings.

As excited as we were, particularly Violet, we decided some restful sleep was in demand. It was already mid afternoon. Tomorrow we could start fresh and renewed. Dove of Spring agreed without argument.

The hotel accommodations were excellent. "Thank you Carlos,"

The hotel actually did not appear to be much different then in the states. I guess that was bound to happen, what with all the world traveling these days.

Rest, food, and more rest was the order of the day. Neither of us objected. Tomorrow would begin a totally new adventure.

~~~~~~
~~~~~~

Up early, well rested, a fantastic breakfast and we were on our way. First stop the three major pyramids.

Our guide, Ohmah, pointed out all the normal tourist stuff which we pretended to listen to. I think we knew more than he did and we were never here before. But he was a most congenial person who was seriously attempting to help.

Dove of Spring and I walked all four sides of each pyramid, counting steps and gaging angles to the top as we did in the jungle. We, naturally, were comparing things to the Maya construction. In my opinion totally as a layman the Maya building appeared to be more sound. Obviously their hidden walls and rooms were far more advanced than their counterparts here in Egypt.

The big tourist attraction of the three great pyramids was indeed laid out according to the constellation Orion, both in distance and offset angles. That alone we found to be an amazing feat considering the dates of construction.

The day was almost dragging on with the normal tourist attractions but we did manage to inquire about a library or something similar so that we may do some reading and research.

Ohmah was most cooperative but did think our request a little strange. Most tourists wanted to see the sights not just read about them. We chose not to explain our motives. He would not understand. I think he just accepted us as a little strange.

Ohmah kept to his word and brought us to a library of sorts. Well, it wasn't a library per se`, but an official agency of the government for serious scientists and archeologists to further their research and / or contribute their findings.

The place was amazing. Isles and isles of books and research papers. A photo archives room as an adjunct to the research papers. We both instantly knew where we would be spending a lot of time. Oh we knew that there were a lot of actual tombs and monuments to see and we planned to see them all.

Dove of Spring had that inspired look again. She was already lost in her own mind. To bring her back to the real world I jokingly suggested that we should have brought along Mr. Blue.

First things first. We thoroughly checked on the

business open hours and to what extent the material was available. Much to my surprise we had free rein to all materials housed here. Plus, they offered any assistance we might need in looking for specific documents. On that point we would hold our own judgement on what we were looking for. After all, what we were looking for was totally out of the ordinary. Who would believe in this day and age a descendant of Nefertiti looking for her heritage.

It was Violet's decision to pass on this today, which surprised the hell out of me. Her reasoning did make sense though. It was already mid afternoon, so why not see some more physical sights and then tomorrow we can spend the whole day reading and researching Also she wanted to organize the notes and facts she had already accumulated from our prior readings. That engineering mind at work again I guess.

Sight seeing we did for the rest of the day. The monuments and statues and wall carvings were endless. So many were aged and weather worn they were totally undecipherable. Though we already knew many people and hours were engaged on the study and translation, or at least partial decipherment of these carvings.

All in all we felt it was a very enlightening and educational day.

Another excellent dinner and we spent the entire evening thoroughly enjoying each others company along with some pleasing Cognac. We never did get to any paperwork.

Up early again, at least Dove of Spring. When I finally did awaken, Violet was already arranging her notes in a more useful order. Her loving smile really brought me to life. It's funny though, all I could see was the Golden Lady and I liked what I was seeing. Deciding to be a little more serious I did get up and shower and joined my Love in organizing paper work.

Our plan was to first ask about Akhenaten trying not to be obvious about our curiosity of Nefertity.

We were immediately directed to the section that covered the eighteenth Dynasty. This is when Akhenaten ruled upper and lower Egypt. This was a new name to both of us. We accidently discovered the name from our original readings back on the reservation. Whispering Wind even had this name underlined in his collection of Egyptian papers. Nefertity was the wife of Akhenaten.

My Dove of Spring was all aglow again and was trying not to show it. I smiled and was happy for her. We both set to reading and digesting all we could on Akhenaten, his reign and naturally any mention of Violet's long ago ancestor.

Time whizzed by and late afternoon was here unexpectedly. We each had a book full of notes. I even surprised myself at not being tired or bored with all that reading and double checking of notes. From the looks of Violet she was ready to continue. She appeared disappointed that it was closing time, which of course, we had no control over. Happy and upbeat we arranged for a return visit.

We were anxious to compare notes yet both agreed we had plenty of time for that. Dinner first at a wonderful restaurant.

Leaving the eatery just at dusk was settling on the pyramids brought visions to us both of the jungle and desert structures. It was an invitation for an evening walk under the stars, particularly the constellation Orion. Seeing it displayed over the pyramids was a breathtaking event. Absolutely mesmerized we totally ignored time and people. We were in our own world. A world of peace and harmony.

Out of no where our original guide, Ohmar, approached us , cautioning us of the late hour and that we should not be wandering the streets at this hour. It was like a wake up call for the both of us. Embarrassed yet laughing we paid attention to his well meaning advice and headed for the hotel. The hotel and a well earned glass of Cognac. Today was almost as tiring as our jungle love.

Home and safe Dove of Spring was floating on air she was so happy.

"**I** just know we are going to have success here. I'm more than positive we will find Nefertiti, no matter what all these reports said about her just vanishing from the records. Akhenaten reigned for many years and she was always mentioned about being forever at his side."

"**D**on't rush it, my love. I'm sure you are right but remember we have been here only two days. Slow your engine down and we will accomplish what we came to do."

Smiling and slightly embarrassed, Violet gave in to my more sensible approach.

"**I** know you are right and you hereby have my permission to keep a tight rein on me. Now how about another Cognac."

Complying with her wishes I joined her in a second Cognac and we put aside our notes for the night.

~ ~ ~ ~ ~ ~

Both with positive attitudes upon awakening the next day we agreed to forego further research for the day to do some more sight seeing which actually was research in itself.

We headed for the city of Amarna, or at least its original location. This was a place designed by Akhenaten to be his home ruling place. A place of peace, rest and tranquility where he could rule under the protection of the Sun Disc. A place for family and protection. The thought was to possibly garner further information of Nefertiti.

Eric and Violet already knew that she had six daughters and was well liked by the people. Over the years of her husband's reign Nefertiti was know by many names.

The Loveliest of Women, True to family and children, Her Beauty Endures, Exquisite Beauty of the Sun Disc, and of course the most famous known, The Beautiful One is Come.

Chapter 5

Amarna turned out to be a bit of a disappointment. There was nothing left but ruins. Over the years there has been many excavations and expeditions of study to find location of Nefertiti's burial and her apparent vanishing act from the public's eye. Nevertheless Eric and Violet made like tourists and studied what they could, looking for the slightest clue or indication of her name. Of course there were numerous carvings and etchings and painting of the royal family but even these were all but obliterated by age, weather and ignorant treasure seekers.

The pair, did however, have a slight advantage over the average tourist. They were both accustomed to minute detail on carvings and markings and being able to read signs easily passed over by most. Their jungle and desert experiences were to their advantage.

Eric even managed to photograph a few marks of interest for further study. After many hours of eye strain they left this once great city and returned to their hotel.

For the next four days they were like other tourists. Taking in the sights everywhere. The valley of the Kings and the valley of the Queens were high on their list and many hours were devoted to their detailed searching and studying.

There were also many other so called burial places of Kings and Queens and family through out the area. Many miles of area. Small pyramids, unfinished tombs, scattered statuary and rock carvings with names and pictures, unfortunately most of the better art works were already in private collections and museums all over the world. The most famous of the beauty of Nefertity was in Berlin, Germany. Adolph Hitler was known for his passion of anything Egyptian.

"The Loveliest of Woman" has been admired for centuries all over the world. This was Dove of Spring's legacy.

Much to her self caused embarrassment and there were many people, tourists and professionals alike, who starred at her as if recognizing her. This, of course, was due to the unmistakable likeness to the beauty of Nefertity.

A few professional archeologists even verbally expressed their belief in the resemblance.

Violet finally had a prepared professional answer for such a thing.

"Why that's impossible. I was born unto the Navaho Nation in the western United States. I have never even been to Egypt before this week."

Then she would laugh it off.

Down deep inside Eric was aware this bothered her, yet she appeared to be taking it in stride. She was proud of her Navaho heritage and obviously proud of her connection to the Golden Lady which in turn led to Nefertity.

I decided for both of us that we had enough for one day and that a relaxing evening was in order. Surprisingly Violet did not argue. In fact, once back at the hotel she was truly just plain old Violet. I was once again happy for her.

The evening was totally relaxing while we quietly discussed future plans.

Dove of Spring even mentioned the frequent occurrence of the Orion markings. I also was aware of the constant reference. There was never any mention or explanation of this frequency. I'm sure most people were not even aware of such markings. But they were special to us and ,of course, our Maya friends.

An early evening and some much needed rest found us up with the sun raring to go. Today's plan was to visit the Sphinx and other unfinished excavations.

The sphinx itself was most impressive when you think about its age. Not only its size but its shape and carving techniques.

Here again is something that baffles the mind. Such a thing today would be quite an undertaking even with our modern technology. How was this achieved ? Also the fact that it is aligned with the winter solstice is mind boggling.

Violet and I chose not to dwell on these things, we had different priorities.

She brought to my attention from her readings that there is a hidden chamber, a rather large one, beneath the feet of the lion facing the solstice direction. This, of course, has not been proven yet, nor has there been any attempt at such an undertaking or excavation.

Strangely enough the fact of a possible hidden room caught Violet's attention. I could tell she was suddenly in another world as she circled back and forth at the feet of the lion. Suddenly I detected a small smile of satisfaction. Looking at me she knew I caught on to her sly smile.

"You felt something, didn't you ?" I quizzed.

"You know me too well my love," was her answer. "There is a chamber there. I just know there is. I'm just surprised that there has been no attempt at an excavation."

"Let's face it my Sweet. In today's day and age you just can't go digging around famous monuments without proper researching and permits. Particularly in such a famous tourist location as here."

She smiled and laughed as she answered.

"I hate it when you are so logical and practical. I'm supposed to be the engineer."

"That you are my Dear, but I do so like that hidden talent of yours to find the impossible. How about we get back to Nefertity ?"

"Right you are Eric. Let's try the Valley of the Queens."

~~~~~~
~~~~~~

The valley of the Queens was similar to other popular excavated areas yet different. First off, there were not many marked tombs or as many excavated places. Whether by design or accidentally, who knows. But, just as in the valley of the kings many tombs were empty. It was said that at one time many queens were buried here but moved at a later date. Once again by design or not is any ones guess.

There were a few references to our Nefertity but nothing concrete. Violet let her inner self do the searching. She was receiving no feelings what so ever.

Disappointing? Not actually. She appeared almost pleased. Apparently she had her own inner feeling as to where she would find her heritage.

The day was far from a total loss. There were many, many stone carvings and pictures that caught our attention and as usual referred to star markings and patterns and the ever present Orion.

Off the beaten path so to speak, we found ourselves pretty much alone. We both steered a course to a lonely rubble pile. No particular reason, it just looked interesting. It wasn't actually a dig, more like a dumping ground from other digs. This truly caught Dove of Spring's attention. Circling the area many times she always returned to the same spot. She at last broke our silence.

"Eric, come look at this."

Without her pointing I saw a definite Orion pattern.

"Look closer, and tell me what you see," she suggested.

It took a few minutes but I finally caught on to what she was referencing. The alignment stars of Orion were somewhat indented. Enough that I could put three fingers into the curves without a problem, as I had so many times before. Particularly on the Lost World grounds. This, of course set my mind to working. Was a Lost World site actually here in Egypt as Violet had suggested? Had it been exposed? Did someone walk in it as we had?

I quickly gazed in Violet's direction only to see a soft

coquettish smile that said, "I told you so."

I returned her smile but with a question mark added. We both decided a closer look at these bits of stone was in order. Sure enough the reverse side was flat and the piece I held was only three or so inches thick. If this did, at one time, lead to the "Lost World" it was only an added covering to the door. With any luck we could pursue areas beyond this to see if there were more. It would truly be an almost impossible task

Violet was now at my side with similar thoughts.

"Our biggest problem now is, how do we find where this was taken from. Near by or even miles away?

Smiling, I answered;

"Now we know what we are going to be doing for the next few days."

With her irresistible smile she softly answered as she took my hand.

"You are so good to me."

Just then our sometimes guide Ohmar spotted us and waved hello. A perfect opportunity I thought. Signaling over to where we were I curiously asked.

"All this rubble, where does it come from. Obviously old tombs, but why dump it here?"

Ohmar answered without hesitation.

"OH! The various excavations have no place to put their diggings if they want to keep their excavating clear for work ability. The locals eventually take most of it to use in their own building projects."

Right away my mind was in motion again thinking of all the ancient history that is being lost or has already been lost. This fact reenforced my own thoughts of the reading I had done recently.

Certain pieces of Egyptian history were definite yet there was so much missing in between. This was obviously part of the answer. This and the fact so much was stolen over the millennia that the real history will never be known because of these missing pieces.

This train of thinking led me to recall Whispering

Wind and his artifact collection. He was trying to save the history of his Navaho Nation. Too bad there were not more like him. Like him and the many Maya decedents we met in the Yucatan. Preserving the past because it was the future. It's amazing how this world is actually going in the wrong direction. What they are calling progress today is actually destruction.

"Now who is in another world? Come back to us Eric. We are still here."

Dove of Spring's soft voice finally registered with me. I turned to look at Violet and Ohmar.,

"I'm sorry, I guess I got carried away. Please accept my apologies."

Ohmar just shrugged it off but I could tell Violet guessed at where I was.

Ohmar left to resume his own business leaving Violet smiling at me knowingly.

"Okay my "Chosen One" where do we go from here."

"We go on looking for your Lost World."

"Oh! So now it's my Lost World," she smiled in return.

Taking her hand in his he started to walk.

"Let's just keep looking."

Down side alleys they went. It was obvious they were not well traveled pathways. Not even for the locals.

In the back of Eric's mind the possible dangers of this decision caught on. He really should be worried for Violet's safety. After a hundred feet or so they were definitely alone. Eric was thinking of turning around when Violet's excited voice suddenly captured his attention.

"Look, there it is again."

She was pointing to the Orion outline on a rough hewn stone wall. This time Orion was surrounded by many, many other star patterns to such a degree that they almost obliterated the Orion Belt. Yet to the trained eyes of Eric and Violet it still made its presence felt. Violet immediately drew closer.

"Look Eric, they also are indented."

She almost put her finger into the depressions but caught herself and pulled back. Looking to Eric she questioned with her eyes. He answered quietly.

"I also want to do that, but we must carefully consider the consequences. Remember the other Lost World. Once the door closed that's it."

" I realize that, but if you think about it logically, it does not make sense. We just never pursued a method of opening the door from the inside."

Feeling somewhat foolish Eric admitted that she was correct.

Dove of Spring pleaded in her "Please" sound. Eric looked around and slowly voiced.

"This is not exactly a very private place as our reservation site."

Having nothing to do with the present circumstances Violet was more pleased to Eric's mention of "our reservation," but chose not to mention it. This was not the time or place. Eric continued his out loud thinking

"What if I do try to open this wall ? What if it does open ? What if it is another Lost World site. ? What about the door closing ? What about other people seeing the door open ? Such an underground sight may be shocking to the uninitiated person. Then what ? How do we explain our presence here ? Last but not least, where is the king when I need him the most ?"

Violet laughed softly as she smiled.

"I'm out of breath from just listening to you and, of course, you are correct as always."

Now even Eric was laughing.

"Now, to throw caution to the wind, try this for size. I will attempt the three finger opening. If it opens, you enter and explore for one hour, no more. I will then open the wall again for your return to me. If this is a success, we will work accordingly from there."

"You would really let me go alone ?" She asked with a puzzling tone.

Smiling now, Eric answered.

"Yes, my Queen. From our past experiences there is no danger in that world of wonder. The only real danger will be if I forget to open the door again."

As he finished, he automatically said ouch, expecting another spousal abuse swat on his arm.

Instead Violet softly answered.

"Then I will just have to stay there in that wonderful world. Who knows, I may just meet another Chosen One to make me happy."

It was now Eric's turn to swat her on the arm while they both laughed.

Calming down and becoming serious Eric took the lead.

"Let's not rush into this," cautioned Eric. "True, this alley appears devoid of people right now but is it always this way? Do we really want others to know of the Lost World yet? If others know, what kind of damage would it do to us, to the Lost World, to this whole area. How many people in today's world would believe. Let's face it, we are in an extreme minority when it comes to Ancient Civilizations. The reigning paradigm would sluff this off as another hoax because it goes against their teachings. Let's go back to the hotel and let this rest awhile."

Violet shook her head in agreement with the words.

"I hate it when you are so logical. Let's remember how to get here and in the meantime keep looking for Nefertity."

"Right you are, my Queen."

They held hands as they quietly left the alley.

Finally walking amongst people again Eric suggested they return to that official and most helpful information center. Violet did not disagree and even suggested they be more direct in asking about Nefertiti. In a round about way of course, yet still more direct than the other day.

An hour later they were settled at a private table with

many books referencing Nefertiti. They read, took notes yet actually came up empty handed. Dove of Spring was obviously disappointed. To the point that she decided to just throw caution to the wind and just ask outright. But even this she did as innocently as possible.

"It appears that many of the past Queens were buried with their spouse rulers or at least close by yet there seems to be nothing about Akenaten's Queen Nefertiti"

The answer she received was most willingly given.

"Yes, Nefertiti was with her King for a while but for some reason unknown at the time was moved to another honored tomb. Then moved yet again for reasons again unknown. The records are vague at this point, and over the centuries became forgotten. We really do not know about her final resting place. Possibly near Amarna There is no way of telling any more."

Violet took this disappointing news in stride as a researcher yet down deep inside knew she would locate her missing legacy.

They thanked the staff for their help and Violet, believe it or not, left on a high note even though she received no solid answers. Eric could not believe her more than good mood and out look without concrete answers.

Once outside Eric questioned Violet on her acceptance behavior. She accepted their answers without getting an actual answer.

"Oh but I did my Chosen One. As you have certain insights in the jungles of the Yucatan, it appears I have acquired those same kinds of insights here in Egypt. It won't be long now and I will find Nerertity I am so glad that we came here. Now I can truly put to rest my unanswered inquisitiveness. I will in fact, know who I am. Both in this world and in prehistory. You my love are the best thing that could have happened to me despite my strong doubts of you when we first met. Fate has put us together. The world is now ours. Both worlds. I am no longer jealous of the Golden Lady. She has actually bought us together."

Here she paused slightly embarrassed.

"Forgive me Eric, I guess I'm letting my emotions get to me. Let's have a good dinner tonight and some wine with dinner, if that's allowed here.

Dinner with wine was superb. They retired for the evening with nothing but high hopes for their future.

~ ~ ~ ~ ~ ~

A relaxing and leisurely start to the day with Dove of Spring deciding on more book and records research. They could resume their physical meandering on the next day. Teller of Stories was amiable to this. His own interest was slowly building. This was quite a change from the Maya history yet at the same time there were similarities to his air photo research. However to him, he felt the air photo work was so much more pleasurable since that his life's work

The staff at this Egyptian resource library were more than pleased by their return to the point one of the staff researched more Akenaten history and many resources were put aside for us. This brought an extremely happy face to Violet. Eric was also pleased though reading book after book was not exactly his thing in life, but he knew how much this meant to his queen. She would do anything for him, so he in turn would do anything for her. Who knows, he figured, it was always good to learn something new.

Believe it or not reading about Akhenaten was very intriguing. He was quite a person and leader. He held his position of leadership for about fifteen years with Nefertiti always at his side. She actually took on the leadership rule in his absence. He initiated the one God system in Egypt. He set up the Sun Disc as the only God.

Resting his eyes for a moment Eric noticed Violet, who appeared to be in a dream state. She had open books in front of her but not reading them. Softly, not to startle her, he whispered; "Come back to this world my love or at least let me join you, where ever you are."

A few seconds passed and she smiled and turned to him apologizing with her eyes only.

I was just reflecting on the time I first met you. I did not trust your motives. I thought you were out to make a fast buck at the expense of my people. Then Lone Buffalo shared your journals with me. After reading from the beginning I thought you were a complete lunatic. Then came the part of talking to the king via ESP. This still rang bells of doubt. Then you even topped that when you were still talking to Atl after he passed from this life. Now I knew you were Wacky!

With all that working against you I still fell in love with you. Then my own life started to change. I knew Whispering Wind my whole life, yet he became a whole other person when you arrived to my people. He, too was talking with his mind and eventually the two of you changed my life again. I never was a student of the paranormal until I met you."

Here Eric interrupted Violet.

"Whoa, slow down love. Why all of a sudden with the one man's confession?"

Violet blushed slightly and softly apologized.

"I almost don't know how to say what I'm about to say."

She paused and showed an embarrassed look.

"Well------- as you talked to Atl and Whispering Wind, I too just received words, at least in my mind, from the Queen herself."

"You mean Nefertiti herself don't you? Why should you consider that strange. She has been occupying your second sense for some time now. Accept what is real. Your lives are now intertwined as one. I am pleased for you. Join the club of crazy people."

She smiled at his last remark, hesitated a bit then continued baring her mind.

"Like the others, Nefertiti was also speaking in riddles."

Eric quietly interrupted. "So that's the connection."

Looking a bit confused Violet asked quietly;

"What connection?"

Eric smiled now knowing he could speak all his thoughts with his soul mate.

"The Riddle." he answered. "I believe it was Diego who explained the use and reason for riddles. The Maya teachers used this method as a tool. Thinking out or being thorough of the reasoning of riddles further implants the subject matter in one's mind. Once learned, never forgotten, so to speak. I must admit though I was getting tired of Atl's riddles but thinking is learning and I did learn. As you well know, you helped with some of them."

"You saying that makes me feel better." Violet said with a smile. "I thought I was going crazy like you and your Maya friends."

"Join the club. Now you are a full fledged member." he answered with a half laugh. "Will you share your riddle with me?"

Giving a thoughtful smile she lovingly answered.

"Of course, my love. I hold no secrets. This is what my mind received."

Dove of Spring slowly repeated word for word what was placed in her mind.

"The world you seek is near as am I. I have been there before. Only true believers will find it. Do not give up your quest. It is closer than you think. The obvious is oft overlooked. Where you seek rest it will be."

There was a short silent pause.

"The hotel" Eric blurted out somewhat startling Violet.

"What about the hotel," she asked quickly.

"Where you seek rest," he continued. True the rooms where we are staying are relatively new, but have you noticed the entire structure is quite aged. I'm willing to bet the Lost World is right under the hotel or at least near by."

Violet was all smiles now.

"Of course and that would answer the riddle. Now I

feel foolish."

"Don't be. It took me a long time to solve some of the king's riddles. As we have said before, between the two of us we can do anything." They hugged in agreement.

Leaving the alley they promised to return and further investigate. Eventually arriving to the hotel, Eric put on the facade of a typical tourist. And enquired of several of the hotel personnel about the age of the building. The answers he received were just what he expected.

"At one time, centuries ago, this rock foundation had apparently been some sort of burial tomb. But age and weather destroyed what ever engraving there was to identify whose tomb it was. Remember sir, we are talking about many centuries. Apparently it had been significant to a few of the higher echelon of dignitaries. No one knows for sure and records of old are very sparse."

This information was exactly what Eric wanted and needed. Still being the tourist he and Violet returned to their room. Here they planned the next day's activities and that was to conduct a thorough inspection of the entire hotel grounds.

"I know we will find the answer."

"Which is?" queried Violet.

"Egypt's Lost World. Or should I say our Lost World." Smiling now he finished with, "Now how about a nice comforting dinner?"

~~~~~~

The morning came sooner then expected for Eric. He still wanted a little more sleep. The last few days caught up to him. Violet did not push and let him have another few hours.

She in the meantime kept reviewing both his and her own notes. She was committed to finding Nefertiti with a confidence she did not know she had.

While Eric was still sleeping Dove of Spring turned her thoughts to the Golden Lady. She remembered the similarities of
~~~~~~

her beauty and that of Nefertiti and not meaning to be vain, recognized her own facial similarity. The only exception being that she, herself, did not have the elongated upper scull. This was not uncommon with the ancient Maya and obviously the Egyptians. The Golden Lady's presence here in the western hemisphere is without a doubt, proof of travel between continents, no matter what the so called experts say. The similarities of astronomy, the pyramids, the Orion alignment and who knows what else, just gives us validation of a Maya-Egyptian connection. The big question is, who came first?

Violet put the notes aside, she felt like she was just confusing herself. She wanted too many answers too quickly. She remembered Eric's words, "Patience and all will come to you."

Speaking of Eric, it's about time he got up.

"I wish I could make the sound of the howler monkeys. That I know would get him up."

Instead, smiling to herself she leaned down and kissed his cheek.

Eric groaned a little then softly said; "Who's that?"

Where upon Violet swatted his arm and turned away.

"Here we go again with the abuse. Are all marriages like this?"

The next thing he knew there was a pillow tossed at him. Both were laughing now.

"If you really want abuse, I can and will oblige you," Violet threw out.

"And I'll bet you could," Eric answered. Then added, "I hope we never get to that stage, My Love."

"We never will, My Chosen One, that I promise. Now how about the Lost World ?"

"Let me freshen up and off we go," replied Eric scooting out of bed.

Violet smiled and proceeded to pick up her notes and put them neatly away. While waiting for Eric a strange feeling over took her psyche. She suddenly sort of froze in place. It was almost as if she sensed a presence although she knew she was alone. Then she sensed the soft voice she heard earlier.

"The world you seek is all around. The portal however is above the ground. Reach for the stars to be underground. The more you look up the deeper the world. You must go up to be able to go down. Fear not the world around you, they know not where you go."

Violet sensed she was alone again. She had not moved, the notes still in her hands. Her inner self was totally pleased. She was confident that was the voice of Nefertiti. She felt her whole being was now smiling. This is what she had been longing for, searching for ever since the Golden Lady contact.

"This is truly the culmination of her life's search," she said to herself.

Eric exited the bathroom to see the ever beautiful smile on his Queen, yet he sensed that she was in another world at this moment.

"I'm glad for her, at least now she won't be throwing any more pillows at me."

He chose not to disturb her and went on to getting dressed for the day's adventures.

Eric accidently knocked a book off the table which, of course, broke Violet's self imposed trance. She was not shocked by the thud but was fully awake now and still smiling.

"Are you that happy to see me," he asked jokingly.

Ignoring his comment she quietly answered.

"I just heard from her. She spoke to me Eric. I actually heard her words. I knew I would find her. I just knew I would," she said still beaming.

Recalling Atl's first contact with him, he knew the sensation she was feeling. He chose not to question her but let her tell her story in her own way. After all he had been through the same thing years ago in the Yucatan.

Ever yet beaming she continued speaking.

"**T**he Lost World, Eric. It is right here. We may be right on top of it for all we know. I will repeat what Nefertiti just told me."

Hesitating for a moment, then with obvious confidence she repeated word for word her ancestor's words. She restated the last sentence with a confident smile.

Now Eric joined her in her smile.

"**I**'m ready! Are you?" he questioned.

Realizing she was still clutching her notes she fumbled to get up and dropped everything.

"**A**llow me my wonderful Queen," Eric voiced as he retrieved the papers.

"**Y**ou must think of me as a child right now."

"**O**n the contrary my Queen. I'm loving you even more. Now let's go find the Lost World."

As they left the hotel turning down a side alley, the ever happy Violet, still in another world, repeated again;

"**I** heard her voice. She actually spoke to me."

Once behind the hotel proper they could view the older rocks and tomb structure that were now the foundation for the main building of the residence.

Eric, now paraphrasing Nefertiti's words sort of mumbled out loud, "We must look up to go down." Both he and Violet were now concentrating their collective gaze upwards. Violet was the first to spot the Orion constellation. It was engraved on an old section of the foundation structure. Not of the hotel itself but most likely an original burial tomb. It was obviously a left over remnant that was more than a burial tomb. This was secreting the entrance to the "Lost World".

"**T**his is just as bad as the King's tomb in the Yucatan," muttered Eric out loud. He looked at Violet who appeared confused.

"**T**here is no way to climb up there safely," she answered.

"**Y**ou are correct in that assumption, my love, but we

can climb down to it safely."

Now Violet was really confused.

"Follow me," Eric said as he started moving to his left around the tomb structure.

Dove of Spring followed without hesitation. She learned long ago to trust Eric's intuition. They both quickly checked the alley for others but luckily they were alone.

Smiling to herself Violet repeated her ancestor's words;

"Fear not the world around you, they know not where you go."

Eric lead the way around to the far side of their goal and sure enough they were shown an easy climb to just above the Orion markings. Ledges, almost like steps, showed the way down. As luck would have it there was also a ledge large enough for both to stand while Eric applied three fingers to the wall. Surprisingly silent the rock parted allowing a narrow entry. Just inside there was already a small boulder near the opening.

"How convenient," Eric thought. "Nothing like planning ahead."

They closed the wall to a crack just large enough for the resident rock. The usual dark surrounded them as Violet reached for Eric's hand. They moved no more than six feet when the mystery lighting came on. Pale though it was, it did illuminate enough the descending steps. Violet could already smell the cool refreshing air scented with flowers and evergreen.

Just as in the other Lost Worlds we were suddenly confronted with the forever blue. Before us was pretty much the same as the other Lost Worlds. As usual I went one way while Violet chose the opposite direction. Almost instantly my interest was peaked. Here before me was again the King's pyramid tomb from the Yucatan. Not more than ten feet from there was the duplicate structure that housed the "Golden Lady."

These similarities were really getting to me now. I was thoroughly convinced of an ancient and highly advanced civilization. It was an obvious forerunner of both the Egyptian and

Mayan culture. There were just too many similarities for this not to be a fact. I had already done some reading of the Central America and Yucatan peoples, yet since here in Egypt with Dove of Spring I had truly done an extensive amount of study of these similarities. Strictly written from only an Egyptian historical record, I was still finding an extreme amount of things alike. Not just math and astronomy, but every day teachings and the working ways of life and death were exactly alike. Far too many to be mere coincidence.

There has to have been a common teacher. Not just hundreds of years but more like thousands of years ago. Atl's chosen ones were most likely their teachers or at least representatives of this advanced culture.

Today's world and studies of ancient history seems to be quite limited. That and the non-acceptance of facts right before their eyes of the so called settlement of the planet.

"Whoa , Slow down boy. You can't convince the present world of things that you have been enlightened with in the last few years. As a "Chosen One" you now know what Atl must have been up against along with his Egyptian counterparts."

Eric forced himself to clear his mind, at least for now.

Dove of Spring, however, was in her glory wandering about this slightly different version of the "Lost World". Basically it was the same as the other two mystery worlds, the only difference being the hidden mini structures.

Off the normal pathway among the floral displays she came upon a mini Amarna, Akhenaten's ruling city built to his liking.

Violet was smiling outwardly now knowing she was close to her dreams fulfillment. She suddenly felt a sense of familiarity with this miniature complex. She circled it many times in both directions. One location in particular seemed to excite a warmth in her more so than the others. She studied this spot carefully. It may have been the location of her tentative burial tomb, but based on her readings there was no guarantee of that.

Violet instinctively knew she would find her soul mate. Who knew, only a few years ago Violet was just a Navajo woman with an engineering degree, and now was part of a world wide history. A history of great importance as far as the development of the worlds advanced knowledge.

Violet suddenly recalled, as she studied this doll house version of Amarna, that Nefertiti was the first female pharaoh. She reigned under quite a different a name which, to Violet, was totally unpronounceable.

ANKHKHEPRURG- SMENKHKAREDJESRKHEPERU

She felt herself swell with pride as she recalled this important piece of information unknown to most of today's population.

Now totally absorbed in her own little world, she lost track of all time and place of being.

Violet started wandering further into this make believe Lost World. She had never done this prior at either of the other two Lost Worlds. She found herself now meandering in a forest area. She could not recall anything like this before. She was not even upset by her present situation but was becoming even more curious. There was no thought of Eric with curiosity now ruling her mind.

Out of nowhere there appeared a small pyramidal structure she guessed to be about seven or eight feet to the tip. A not quite hidden door showed itself, Orion cluster of stars and all. Without hesitation she moved to the door and pressed the three indented stars. Sure enough, the soft sound of stone on stone echoed as the door center pivoted open.

She hesitated not but slipped through the narrow opening. The door softly closed behind her. Panic did not show itself. That was the farthest thing from her mind. Curiosity truly reigned.

Two steps forward into the dark and the usual magic light system glowed showing a long descending corridor. Suddenly Eric came to mind.

"He will just love this," she thought, yet still did not concern herself that she was alone.

Violet continued onwards yet again marveling at this tunnel with its highly polished walls. She took the few zigs zags in stride not really paying attention to time. She had not noticed anything unusual, such as wall markings or Glyphs on the walls. That is until she was confronted with a stone wall blocking her passage, which did have markings on it. She also could detect seams. After all Eric had taught her a lot over the last two years. On closer inspection, sure enough she could make out the Orion complex.

"**I** wish Eric were here now," she said aloud.

In a quiet whisper so as not to startle her too much Eric answered:

"**O**h but I am here now."

Dove of Spring was startled a touch but recovered quickly when she saw Eric.

"**H**ow did you get here?" they both said simultaneously.

Now laughing they each said for the other to go first. Eric took the offer.

"**W**hy? I don't know but this small structure, like a mini pyramid was suddenly in front of me. It was only about six or seven feet tall. It sort of begged me to enter. I even remember saying to myself, "Violet will just love this." Well, I entered it and here I am with my true love."

On hearing the last few words Violet kissed his cheek.

"**N**ow, I may ask what you are doing here?"

"**T**he exact same situation you just outlined, and here I am."

"**D**idn't you think you were taking a chance alone?"

"**B**elieve it or not that thought never entered my mind. I guess my curiosity took over my mind. Now what do we do?'

"**W**ell, you were going to try this doorway, don't stop on my account."

Smiling now Violet pressed three fingers on the appropriate marks and the familiar sound could be heard as the wall pivoted. The usual dark passageway greeted them. They looked at each other hesitatingly.

"**W**ell, you were going to do this alone, so lead on my

"Queen," as Eric stepped aside bowing and waving his arm to the passage way.

Violet hesitated no longer and stepped into the darkness. Within six feet of movement the miracle illumination they had grown accustomed to showed the way to what appeared to be a never ending passage. They followed quietly, both with eyes ever searching the walls for signs of entry ways or Glyph's for information. The results to date were negative. No words were exchanged. The tunnel seemed endless, yet they continued onward. Passage of time or distance traveled had no meaning. The pair were obsessed with discovery.

Approximately two hours of wordless search and follow passed when suddenly distant voices could be detected. Eric and Violet searched each others eyes questioningly. It was almost as if the voices were familiar. Both quickly dismissed this idea from their minds. They continued on at a slightly slower pace still hearing familiar voices.

A short distance ahead appeared a pivoted doorway slightly ajar. This is where the voices were the strongest. The same thought struck both Violet and Eric at the same time. The voices were familiar yet neither wanted to believe what they were hearing.

Forward motion now halted they listened more intently. This was Diego's voice beyond doubt, but this was quite impossible. It can't be.

Eric thought back to his earlier research and recalled the distance between Egypt and the Yucatan was roughly seventy two hundred miles, plus or minus. He did not have his notes with him for the exact miles. He quickly dismissed these thoughts allowing for his overactive imagination.

"I think it's time I had some grounding," he thought to himself. He no longer finished thinking when Violet , in a bewildered voice remarked,

"I could have sworn that was Diego's voice yet I know that's impossible."

"I was thinking the same thing yet I know that's totally implausible."

Eric nodded to the opening and Violet led the way

as she squeezed through the narrow space followed by Eric. They were determined to pursue this strange tunnel to who knows where.

The all too familiar Glyph appeared now and again indicating the air vent system. Apparently this air vent system was constructed along the same lines as the Yucatan system. Perhaps by a common intelligence of the Lost Civilization. Eric no longer had doubts that such an advanced peoples did live and were trying to teach us. It seems though, that modern day mans ignorance and refusal to learn won out.

There I go again, getting carried away with my thoughts. Pay attention Eric, to what you are doing.

Violet, however was steadfast in her determination.

No more than twenty minutes slid by when the pair saw another door already opened. The same voices could be heard. As Violet passed through the opening she immediately stopped with Eric running into her.

Two voices could be heard simultaneously including the echoes.

"What are you doing here?"

It was Diego along with Mateo who immediately spoke.

"I thought you two were not coming to the Yucatan this Year."

"We are not, we are in Egypt. What are you doing in Egypt?" answered Violet instantly.

"We are not in Egypt. We are at the King's tomb as always in Frank's lost city. All four of us are here as usual."

Teller of Stories and Dove of Spring searched each others face and eyes not believing what they were seeing or hearing.

Diego finally spoke out;

"Okay you guys, enough with the jokes. When did you get here and why didn't you tell us you were coming."

Violet, almost in a commanding position, put her hand up indicating silence. All eyes turned to her.

"Here again we are faced with a wondrous mystery of the Lost Civilization. A fact that is obviously beyond comprehension."

Now we all looked confused, including Violet, yet she did put forth an explanation almost beyond our understanding. She smiled now saying she would explain her thoughts.

"What we are all now experiencing is beyond our logical thinking as scientists."

Dove of Spring asked Diego directly.

"How long, time wise, did you travel to get to this point?"

Diego, still a bit confused, hesitated, then answered.

"I guess it was about an hour and a half"

As he said this he looked at Mateo who shook his head affirmatively.

"We also have traveled approximately two hours from our hotel in Egypt."

She emphasized the ***EGYPT.***

"Yet here we are together. If this does not answer, with positive proof, the past existence of an older, extremely advanced civilization, then I'm going back to the reservation and weave blankets for the tourists."

Of course she ended with a smile.

We were all silent just staring at her. Suddenly from behind Diego and Mateo clapping could be heard. Carlos and Mario had joined us. After the hello's and back patting we settled down to some serious discussion.

"How do you make a distance of some seventy two hundred miles over the face of the planet be traveled in three or four hours underground. Even drawing a straight line through the globe itself you are still looking at many thousands of miles. You, my Queen may be on to something," Carlos put forth.

All eyes now focused on Carlos, confused though they were. Carlos continued.

"The tunnel you just came from I assume was from a Lost World you found in Egypt, correct?"

Both Eric and Violet nodded affirmatively.

"As did we from the Lost World we all discovered

here in the Yucatan."

Here Eric interrupted but with a smile.

"You just said here in the Yucatan yet we're saying in Egypt. How can this be?"

"You are right about that, but I think I have an explanation for that. It's a little far out but it would help explain this conundrum."

Diego, in his usual light air broke in with;

"You guys are testing the weird hypophysis again. Art is so much simpler but go ahead, I'll just listen."

Of course we all laughed.

Scientists, recently have been discussing the factual existence of worn wholes in space. I know this sounds ridiculous, but as we have seen so far, this lost Civilization was far more advanced than we are, even now. What if they were able to make use of the worm hole theory here on earth. That would explain traveling huge distances in a comparatively short time. Hence this tunnel system. We each traveled three thousand plus miles to meet here in only two and one half hours. How do we account for that, never mind anybody believing us. We are witnessing and are part of an advanced science beyond our present day comprehension."

Here Mario joined with,

"You're right, it is almost unbelievable but we are part of it right now. I thought the tunnel system in the jungle was amazing but this is truly beyond belief.

Silence reigned for a minute or so interrupted by the soft voice of Dove of Spring.

"If this Lost Civilization was this advanced so many centuries ago, What happened to them? Where are they? Why are they not here?"

"Never mind that now," Eric joined. "Let's work with what we have. This will help explain the similarities of the Egyptian and the Mayans or even their predecessors, who knows how long these two knew the worm holes were here."

Mario added his own speculations to the discussion.

"So far we have discovered three of these Lost World playgrounds. Are there more? If so how many and where? Are they all connected by these worm hole tunnels? That would really help in understanding the growth of what we now know of as civilization."

Eric sort of gave a frustrated laugh.

"And we no longer have the King or Whispering Wind to riddle us information."

Violet quickly added,

"But we do now have Nefertiti."

She went on to explain to the others her mental conversations with her Egyptian relative, Queen Nefertiti.

Diego, with his usual sideways humor commented,

"And now we have another "talking to the dead" joining the way out weirdo club."

Smiling in answer Violet shot back,

"I couldn't let all you gentlemen have all the fun. That just wouldn't be fair. If it were not for her instructions, Eric and I would not be here right now."

Mario, smiling himself, put up his hand,

"Okay, okay, let's get back to our mystery. Why are we here and how did we get here?"

His comment did have a sobering effect on the group. Now a serious Carlos brought up the obvious.

"We all agree these people of the past were extremely advanced in sciences, mathematics and astronomy, and to get back to Violet's question, what happened to them? Conjecture would dictate that they also were mortal and had a limited life span. That being the case why was not this, so important knowledge, passed on to younger generations? Today, and I'm referring to the last few centuries, we are only now by comparison, testing the waters of this advanced knowledge. We are not the scientific community that is seriously studying the "new" things, but for some reason we have been privy to view this advanced wisdom of the ancients. Again the question "WHY"?

Here he paused so his words could be digested.

On a lighter note Mario, with a serious look turned to Eric.

"See what you started Eric. You and your mental communications with the king. Us being in this quandary is all your fault."

He finished with a smile.

"I guess I should have stayed in Vermont just taking pretty pictures," he answered.

Carlos joined again with,

"As much as you may have liked that, is not this much more challenging. Learning things we don't understand?"

Mateo finally joined the dialogue.

"What good is all this doing for us. We can't tell anybody. Especially the way all this came about. True, there may be a few people that would understand, but they probably would not be listened to either."

"I think we all agree with you on that," interrupted Eric. "But I for one would like to take this as far as we can. Let's face it, this all fits in with the message the king was trying to put forth. He and others, as chosen ones, were trying to teach these very facts and lessons of the Lost Civilization, which, by his own admission fell on deaf ears. We few appear to be the only ones to understand this."

Silence took over for the moment until a soft voice breathed two short words "ICE AGE."

Silence still remained.

"There have been more than one." Carlos brought to mind. "So which one are we referring to. The possibility exists of more than one. Roughly every twelve thousand years plus or minus because of precession."

"I knew you were going to bring that up because I was thinking the very same thing. In some of the Mayan/ Olmec folklore I have read just such a thing is referred to. Not as an ice age per se`, but as a world wide cataclysmic disturbance that wiped out almost everything on the planet, both man and beast. An ice age would certainly fit the bill."

With everyone staring blankly at each other, quiet again took over until a voice of reason was heard.

"Gentlemen," said Violet catching the attention of all.

"Come back to reality. We can not hope to understand the reasoning of those of thousands of years ago, but we can use whatever resources we have to understand ourselves and the situation we are faced with. We cannot change the past let alone understand it, but we can regulate our own future, more appropriately our near future. If we really want to do specific scientific research than I suggest we further investigate other "Lost Worlds" where ever they may be. I realize that none of us here have the time or the money to search the world over for other "Lost Worlds" parks as you referred to them, but why not further investigate such things as the way we all arrived here."

She lingered here before going further. She could tell they were all listening and had followed her every word.

After checking Eric's eyes and receiving a positive nod she continued.

"These worm holes, as you call them, are a bit new to me. I have done some basic reading of them but must admit at the time they did not attract my attention. But you folks seem to be familiar with their principals, so why not pursue that avenue. It may just lead to other parks. It brought us here, so why not to others?"

Here Violet stepped back wearing a half grin.

Carlos, also with a half grin, followed immediately.

"This woman is not only one of us, she is one up on us. She went right to the heart of the matter that we obviously were missing the simplicity of. Of course she is absolutely correct."

"I thank you for that vote of confidence, but..."

Here she lingered with the words but directly recovered.

"Your search of the other Lost Worlds will have to exclude me, or us indicating Eric. I must, at all cost, finish my quest to locate my heritage. Apparently nowhere is recorded the actual burial site of Nefertiti. There are many possibilities yet nothing is confirmed. I must find out for myself, the world need not know or care. We, Eric and I will join in the search once I am personally satisfied. I'm sorry to be a party pooper."

"Your personal pursuit is as important as ours. We would not ever stand in your way," offered Mario. "But we do look forward to your assistance in our future quests."

"That makes me happy to hear that and if I can contribute in any way it would be my pleasure. For now you go play with your worms, Eric and I should return to Egypt and continue my quest. I wish you luck."

Eric, hand in hand with Violet started their journey back to their hotel. Eric yelled over his shoulder; "We will be in touch very soon."

The four Mayan researches also called it quits and started their own journey back to the Yucatan each realizing there was a lot of reading to be done if they ever wanted to understand the worm holes throughout the universe.

Chapter 6

Not really paying attention to the distance traveled, both Violet and Eric admitted they had enough exercise for one day. Dinner, shower and a good nights sleep were in order. Both readily agreed.

Back at their starting point they faced the closed doorway.

"Now what?" posed Violet. "You always had your shoe in the other doors."

"Not only that but the other "Lost Worlds" were in the middle of nowhere. There was little or no chance of meeting another person."

It was then Violet again recalled the words of Nefertiti.

Her final words were

"Fear not the world around you, they know not where you go."

Accepting that as a go ahead Eric searched for the Orion constellation on the inside of the portal. Faintly etched in the stone were the three stars of Orion's belt. He touched all three together and the ever familiar rolling of stone took place. The opening that showed itself was narrow but enough to let a man pass sort of sideways.

"That's funny," remarked Eric. "I seem to recall upon entering the two of us could pass at the same time."

"Perhaps it was designed that way on purpose," proposed Violet. "Try touching the three stars again. I'm guessing the door will close."

Eric looked at her sort of funny like yet did as she requested. Sure enough the portal was closed instantly.

"To keep out the uninvited," she smiled.

"You really amaze me sometimes," Eric answered.

He touched the marks again and the door opened. He and Violet slid to the outside. As predicted there was not a soul around.

"I'm so hungry I could eat a horse," Eric joked.

"We are in Egypt. Will a camel do?" Violet shot back .

"Do they really eat camels?"

"I don't know," Violet answered . "And I don't want to find out."

~~~~~~

A night of well needed rest found the couple up early and making plans for the next few days.

Eric was not quite sure of directions to go. On the other hand Dove of Spring, had her heart and mind set on returning to Amarna and possibly even seeing the Akhenaten settlement. Deep inside she found it difficult to understand that someone as famous as Nefertiti did not have a final resting place. Her name and likenesses were depicted all over Egypt yet there were no actual recordings of her final burial tomb. Possibilities were investigated but without any final resolutions.

This fact really bothered Dove of Spring. Even this she found to be odd behavior for her. She had always been well grounded in fact. And she led her life that way up until The Golden Lady. It wasn't that long ago that she knew nothing of Nefertiti let alone the ancient history of Egypt and its governing Pharaoh.

The fact that she was a descendent of the famous queen sort of impacted her outlook on things. She just hoped she
~~~~~~

could handle this added pressure. She now totally understood Eric's dilemma of being a "Chosen One" and not by his own choosing. But as they both kept reassureing each other, together they will get through anything.

Eric, as usual, succumbed to Violet's pleading eyes and they headed back to Amarna. They purposely were in touch with their sometimes guide Ohmar, to let him know where they were going. He agreed to keep an eye for their return.

From what they had read on the building of Amarna, it must have been an impressive sight in its day.

Violet wanted to revisit all the building sites again. Eric assumed she wanted a final reassurance that Nefertiti's tomb was not there or perhaps had been destroyed.

They tried to appear as normal tourists but no one was going to interfere with Violet's quest.

We circumnavigated the entire city in extreme detail. She was not to be denied every nook and cranny.

As the day wore on with no positive results, Dove of Spring was becoming more excited by the hour. It was a positive excitement.

At the time I said nothing yet I guessed her mind was already focusing on more positive finds back at the area of Akenhaten.

For her happiness and satisfaction I also truly desired she find what she was pursuing. This whole thing was one hell of a story covering these many thousands of years of related personages. We all have a family tree of sorts, but this is a family forest going this far back in time.

Actually I was jealous of her. Not in a bad way though. To have that kind of family lineage, I think I would also be proud and excited.

I'm lucky I can trace my lineage back to my grandfather and even that's doubtful. Down deep inside I could actually feel her emotions and I am lucky that she shares them with me. The King and Whispering Wind were of great assistance in boosting my ego but Dove of Spring is furthering that because of her heritage. Who could not love such a woman. Thank you Frank

Thurber. This all came about because you invited me to take a few jungle pictures..

Enough of living in the past, let's return to reality.

We had exhausted all of the avenues of discovery and Violet was more than satisfied that her ancestor was not here.

As if nothing had transpired this whole day, and being her old normal self she suddenly stated; "Let's go back to the hotel, I'm starving."

Instantly I laughed at this but agreed whole heartily.

~ ~ ~ ~

"**L**et us reflect a moment. I know I have said this before but we can not change the past. We may not, as only two people, reach to change the future, or for that matter, the present. The only control we have is over our own lives at the present time. I can not even control your thoughts nor can you control mine. We can both influence each other but control is an individual thing. We control only our own destiny."

"**I** did not realize I married such a philosopher. I bow to your insight my "Chosen One."

"**Y**ou are my insight my Queen. First there was the King, then came Whispering Wind and now the Golden Lady which lead to you. My education is ever changing, thanks to you and your legacy."

Our trip back to the hotel was a happy one. Violet appeared very happy with the no results at Amarna. I could tell she would now concentrate on the Valley of the Kings and the city of Akhetaten. This was one very determined lady.

Ohmar spotted our return and inquired about our day and mentioned he would continue keeping us in his range. He said he owed that much to Carlos. I chose not to pursue the Carlos connection. I figured that was his private business.

A wonderful dinner with wine topped off the day perfectly. We now relaxed with some classical music, *"I really missed* *my jungle serenade"* and a welcome snifter of Cognac.

I still could not believe how content and happy Violet was even after that disappointing day. A more positive person I don't think I have ever witnessed. I just accepted her for what she is and I loved her for it.

We had a slow and easy start in the morning. There just seemed not to be a rush. We eventually did make it to the city of Akheteten, or what was left of it. Just like Amarna it was half destroyed, not just by age but by tomb builders and thieves who pillaged from one to build others in other areas. It was obvious where once carved Cartouchs had been chipped away and new names and dates were re-carved for various new favorites of Pharaoh's and their queens. Even those of Akhenaten and his religious Sun Disc displays had been redesigned with graffiti.

A laggardly pace was adopted by Dove of Spring as she carefully inspected every tomb or thought to be tomb in as much detail as she could. Though to me it appeared more like a listening inspection. I chose not to say anything. This was now her world.

Many interesting hours passed and about mid-day Violet suddenly stopped. An unmarked and as yet untouched tomb which appeared in relatively good condition was gathering all her attention. Some barely readable scratching did however show the name Akhenaten. This may have been one of his many resting places. It was known that he had been moved several times.

My own Golden Lady suddenly appeared frozen in place. It was probably my own imagination yet a calm and quiet seemed to reign over the immediate area. The same sort of calm the jungle took on when there was the passing of a large cat crossing the area. Of course this grabbed my attention but not so Violet. She was totally immersed in another world of her own.

I said not a word but took on the role of protector so that she was not disturbed. Rather abruptly her being took on an aura or glow. Not that it could be physically seen but a look I had become familiar with. I made not a sound. Violet's eyes appeared to focus on the ground. She herself took on the appearance of an unmoveable rock.

"I am here my child. Your home is forever with me, as I am forever with you. We are one again. No longer will you have to search or wonder as no longer will I. Go and fulfill your destiny as I did mine. You have a Chosen One by your side. Together you will accomplish much. Do not let others lack of understanding deter you. Your path is right and just as was mine. My pride goes with all your work, success will always be yours. Your task against the world is not and will not be an easy one. Do not get discouraged. Use your past to conquer the future. I am now happy for both of us. Go in peace now my child. Go and fulfill your true destiny."

Thank goodness there were very few people in the area at the time. There was no disturbance of any kind. Time seemed to stand still. Even I do not have any idea how long the time was frozen. I could not and would not take my eyes away from my Queen. I guess even I put myself into a sort of trance. I know the whole world was blocked out of my consciousness.

The next thing I knew Violet had her arms around me in a loving hug as she kissed me with love.

"We can go home now my darling."

She lovingly whispered as she took my hand and led us away from the tomb setting. She was still glowing and I dared not say a word.

Utter silence prevailed for the next couple of hours but I could feel and almost see the consummate happiness vibes emoting from Violet. She was no longer Violet or even Dove of Spring. She was a queen in her own right, descendent of her famous ancestor.

As we neared the hotel the silence was quietly broken as Violet looked up at me with her ever loving smile stating; "We can go home now, my darling and I mean to our real home. Let's check on a flight as soon as possible."

Chapter 7

The many flights home were boring yet again they weren't. We both, in our own way, were reviewing over and over in our minds the many things we learned in Egypt.

My main thrust now was to fit the puzzle pieces of the Lost Civilization and the Egyptian connection to the Maya. I still found it difficult to wrap my mind around a seventy two hundred plus or minus miles distance between Egypt and the Yucatan at a period of thousands of years ago. True we now have positive proof with the "Golden Lady" but we really need more if we expect to convince the world of such a relationship.

The Maya oral history handed down tells of such a relationship. I'm sure there was some written documentation of it also. But unfortunately this was completely destroyed by the Spanish conquest who considered it heretical, not even knowing what it said..

"Oh, if we could only relive history again to correct the mistakes we now know were made out of ignorance. What a world we would have now."

Enough of that, back to reality.

On the very last leg of our journey home, Violet mentioned that one of the first things to do when we reached the reservation was to go to the hogan, now museum, of Whispering Wind. She was positive she would find recorded evidence of the Egyptian connection.

"Great idea, and I would like to review in more detail the Egyptian trade contracts. We should also contact the guys at the

King's tomb."

They both were quiet again until suddenly Eric blurted out "The Ankh" We have the Ankh as proof. I know it is only one thing but it still is physical proof.

Shyly Violet asked; "What's an Ankh?

"It is a quasi religious article possibly symbolizing long or enduring life It is usually made of silver or gold or some other precious metal. It is made sort of like a cross with a handle on it to carry or wave about. It is from ancient Egypt. We have one in what we called the treasure room at the King's pyramid. I believe I did show you the room. That is the room that put Frank Thurber over the edge. He let all those precious items of value get to him. There are literally hundreds of items of great value in that room. I imagine they were either gifts or elements of trade from all over the world. World wide contact many hundreds, if not thousands of years ago. We were the first to open that structure, in we don't really know how many years."

"Okay, my love, calm down." said Violet as she reached for Eric's hand. You will upset the whole airplane."

I was a bit embarrassed and was glad Violet was there to control my outburst.

"We'll go into more detail when we get home with no one else around." I said quietly in return.

Violet smiled and continued to hold Eric's hand

Eric's mind was running amock, as the expression goes. He did calm down with Dove of Spring's loving touch.

As pre-arranged Dan met them at the airport and drove them to the calm and peaceful reservation. Dan was allowed some details but would have to wait for the whole story after the world travelers rested.

Violet's house was a warm and welcome sight.

~ ~ ~ ~ ~ ~

The first full day and night at home was devoted to rest for both mind and body. Nothing Egyptian was openly discussed but each alone were reviewing the past weeks in their own silent ways.

Dan, not really wanting to, left them undisturbed. He knew they would contact him when ready and rested.

The Ankh was constantly on Eric's mind while Violet s focus seemed to be on her Egyptian connection.

On the third night home while resting in the evening in their three tree jungle with their favorite Cognac, they finally agreed they were back to normal enough that they could sensibly and without too much emotion discuss what has happened with their time in Egypt. Violet opened their discussion.

"**I** heard the words of Nefertiti. We stood where she was entombed."

"**I** sensed that much," Eric replied. "I knew how much that meant to you so I let you have your time and space. I still will not push."

"**W**e are so well meant for each other. Too bad the rest of the world doesn't think as we."

"**Y**eah, I think I'll keep you around," Eric smiled in answer. They laughed together.

After a short pause Dove of Spring relayed the Queens message to Eric. Not word for word but the general gist and meaning. Even with the quiet retelling Eric could detect the swelling of pride in his own Queen.

"**O**f course no one in today's world is going to believe this relationship considering the span of years involved."

"**T**hat matters not my love. We and our few Maya friends know the truth. That is all we need. We both know we will never change the world's thinking of what we have discovered these last few years. Perhaps sometime in the future the real story will take hold. But I'm afraid that will be well beyond our time. So don't let it disturb the woman I'm looking at right now."

Violet answered with one of her loving smiles while saying.

"**B**efore I get all teary eyed how about a refill on the Cognac."

Returning with the requested refill Eric went into some more detail of the Ankh and how it could help prove Egyptian contact long before Columbus. He really felt the world's story needed to be rewritten even though it would drastically change history as we now know it.

Violet did not disagree but softly requested they change the subject for now.

"Let's just enjoy the evening and each other. Tomorrow we can start life all over again."

Smiling, Eric went along with the idea and as if reading Violet's mind added

"We can start by revisiting the Lost World. Who knows where hidden tunnels are to lead us to and who knows where."

Violet lit up at the suggestion and smiled.

"We do so belong together."

Their relaxation continued with a third Cognac.

Chapter 8

Lone Buffalo finally had some time and was knocking at the door first thing. Luckily the travelers, now rested, were up and about. Instantly Dan poured forth with questions about Egypt. Violet willingly started their story while Eric prepared the black, syrupy liquid they all liked so well.

The three now supplied with their morning elixer, relaxed while Eric alternated with Violet on the details of their adventure.

"You guys are pulling my leg about this tunnel thing halfway to the Yucatan. That's just not possible. You're talking thousands of miles."

"You're exactly right," answered Eric. "If you want to check on this way out story you can ask your Maya pals."

Smiling now, Dove of Spring joined with

"I did not want to believe it either, but I was there and yes we met Carlos and the others. It seemed we both discovered this additional tunnel in the "Lost World" of each nation."

"This is really hard to swallow. I'll say again are you two pulling my leg?"

"I wish it were a joke," Eric interrupted. "But it isn't. Now this opens up a whole new avenue of thinking."

Violet finished Eric's sentence.

"We are now possibly looking at Quantum theories."

"Whoa, slow down you guys. I had trouble enough with High School algebra, now you want to throw me into another unknown world."

All three were silent for a moment as each sipped their coffee. Eric took the lead.

"I know it sounds far fetched but like it or not that is exactly where we are. Lets review this all from the beginning."

Both Eric and Violet took some time rehashing their tunnel travels and meeting up with the Yucatan group.

It was Carlos who first brought up cataclysms and ice ages., which led to Violet mentioning worm holes, which of course, brought to the fore front Quantum Theories and Physics.

Here, Eric continued alone.

"I know very little of Quantum Physics. By comparison it has only been recently that this subject has been formally studied. It was basically started by Einstein's relativity theory. Yet here we are with what could be an actual working model of such a thing from thousands of years ago."

Eric paused here to let this little bit sink in.

"We apparently have an awful lot of catching up to do."

"The most difficult part of that is how do we approach the world with a working model of something they are only now thinking about, let alone bringing to fruition. By comparison we are thousands of years behind these people who made this "Lost Civilization."

Dan was absolutely quiet. He instinctively knew his friends were telling the truth. He, himself was believing what was just put forth before him.

Right now he just wanted to go back to finding buried pyramids in the desert with Mr. Blue.

Dan slowly stood up excusing himself.

"I'm going back to my class room, I need time to think."

Without another word Eric and Violet understood. This was a lot to digest. They, themselves had not yet accepted what they just outlined. This was quite a hurdle to get over. That was the most exciting part of it all. They wanted to accept the challenge. Naturally what ever they came up with they would share with their friends down in Central America.

~ ~ ~ ~

Both Violet and Eric were silent except for the sips of coffee. Eric thinking of the words just spoken. They totally understood the feelings of Lone Buffalo. They had expressed those same misgivings themselves.

The quiet interrupted only by the song of birds outside went on undisturbed. Eric remembered times like this in the jungle. To him this was a good thing. Violet was having similar thoughts. She too missed the quiet noise of the jungle.

As if on que they both spoke at the same time.

"**W**e should go back to our own "Lost World."

Violet followed with; "Today"

Leaving their unfinished coffee they both arose to prepare for their outing to who knows where.

On the drive to the "Lost world" site Violet expressed both their feelings.

"**W**ho would have guessed our lives would take this kind of turn."

Happily they drove on.

Out of the clear blue Eric, half jokingly voiced

"**I** wonder if Mr. Blue knew about this Quantum tunnel?"

They both laughed but at the same time wondered silently.

Arriving at the now familiar site each questioned what was in store for them. Eric had forgotten snacks and drinks but at this time it mattered not.

Facing the rock wall Eric performed the three finger touch to Orion's belt and the door easily swung open. This time it appeared almost silently. They just chalked this up to their anxious imagination.

Eric started to remove his boots to hold the door open but Violet stopped him.

"Let's check out the door first," she suggested. "Remember the door in Egypt. Perhaps this could be the same."

"And if it isn't we could be stuck here for eternity."

"At least we would be together," she smiled in answer.

With his boots first in place at the door opening they proceeded to check out the inside of the door. Sure enough there was Orion and indications at the three belt stars. Throwing caution to the wind Eric allowed the door to close much to the delight of Violet. Here she took the lead and touched three fingers to the star marks and sure enough the door opened.

Happily Eric put his boots back on saying;

"I was beginning to get scratched up feet in the name of science."

With that Violet swatted his arm again.

"Here we go again," responded Eric laughing.

As they entered the forever blue, Eric spoke out.

"Let's stick together on this trip. I do not want to lose you to this forever world."

Violet liked his words and clasped his hand tightly.

"Yes my "Chosen One" this we do together. If we get totally lost, at least we will be lost together."

"Look out world, here we come," answered Eric.

"Do we take the right path or the left?" asked Violet.

"You always went right and to date discovered more than me, so the right path it is."

On they went, again admiring the perfection of beauty of this "Lost World."

"I just realized the fact that there is not really much difference between this world or the other two that we have seen," mentioned Violet off handedly.

"To me that is just another testament to how

advanced this old world was compared to us right now."

They meandered here and there yet basically kept to the main pathway. Sort of thinking out loud Violet mumbled

"**I** wonder if anyone else is doing this?"

"**D**oing what?" Eric questioned.

"**W**alking around in one of these Lost Worlds as we are and if there are any more."

"**I**'m sure there are a few more. It just stands to reason. They may not have been discovered yet but it's reasonable to assume that there should be. Remember, at one time there were many "Chosen Ones."

"**A**nd there message fell on deaf ears until you came along."

Violet emphasized the you both with her voice and hand squeeze.

"**A**nd now you also," Eric shot back.

Violet finished up with a smile and the words

"**D**on't forget your four Mayan pals and we can add Dan also."

"**P**erhaps there is hope for the world yet, but I doubt we will see anything in our time," Eric answered sadly.

Quickly changing the subject Eric mentioned

"**W**e're here to look not talk, so let's look."

"**Y**es boss," Violet shot back.

Violet suddenly saw a spot between some flowers that appeared wide enough to follow, which she automatically did, her eyes constantly on the move.

She shouted getting Eric's immediate attention. Well hidden under some unidentifiable flowers there was a flat topped pyramid. Eric recognized it right away. It was an exact duplicate of the odd shaped structure that housed the "Golden Lady." He judged this look alike to be about a foot squar and seven or eight inches high. He was struck by the extreme detail to duplicate the original full size one back in the jungle. It even showed the constellation signs on the top four sides. These finds of another world never cease to amaze him. He was so under its spell he failed to hear Violet trying to get his attention.

"What worlds were you in?" she asked when he finally recognized her talking. "This almost looks like one of the buildings back in the jungle," she remarked.

"Not almost," he answered. "It is an exact duplicate. This is where our "Golden Lady" rests," he repeated the name "Golden Lady" with reverence.

Eric continued staring at the small object in silence. Violet could tell by his expression he was deep in thought again. She allowed him time before she interrupted.

"What kind of quandary are you in now my love? I hate seeing you like this. You appear to be seriously upset about something."

He suddenly realized somebody was talking to him. Now out of his trance he recalled her words. More relaxed now he answered.

"I just can't figure out the why of it. Why all these tunnels? Why these hidden "Lost Worlds" as we call them? And now why these miniature replicas of pyramids and such not really native to the areas we are finding them? What is the purpose of all this? The tunnels I can see to hide treasures from the Spanish invaders. Then again the tunnels themselves show an advanced knowledge of construction and earth moving. But at the time of European incursion on South and Central America the methodology for such things did not exist. Yet here we are in the middle of it. Hence the when, where, why and how."

"Wow!" answered Violet. Are you sure you don't have a PHD in everything? That was quite a mouthful. I wish I had an answer for you."

Eric smiled at her.

"Although it does sort of prove that there must have been an advanced peoples on this world who knew how long ago. As the king said so many times, they were trying to teach us but without much success."

Violet moved to her Chosen One enfolding him in her arms.

"Now its up to us to carry on the King's work."

For some reason or another Dove of Spring's words made him feel better. He smiled at Violet while saying

"Well, let's see what else we can find out at this model site. It was not built this way to be pretty."

Violet felt better herself. Eric was back to normal. At least she thought so. He had that questioning look in his eyes again. Sure enough he began mumbling aloud.

The "Lost World" pyramid we found in Egypt at least was tall enough to have an entrance door. This little model is only about a foot high."

His thinking was quietly interrupted by Violet.

"Look!" She said pointing to the top platform. "The Orion Belt stars. At least that's what they look like to me."

Eric now fully alert again glanced to where she was pointing.

"You are absolutely correct. You have done it again. Now I know I have to keep you around."

She was going to swat his arm again but thought better of the idea. This was not the time for levity.

Eric dropped to his knees for a closer look. True enough the complete Orion constellation was marked out on the top platform. It was very faint, but there nevertheless. He lightly brushed his hand over the markings. Sure enough he felt the indentations of the stars of Orion's belt. He hesitated for a moment until he heard the encouraging words from behind him.

"Yes, go ahead."

He gently rested his three fingers on the stars. A few seconds later a soft swishing sound caught their attention about eight feet in front of them. The ground itself was rising. A plot about four feet wide opened, flower bed and all, which did not appear to be disturbed.

"Of course not," thought Eric, *"This advanced culture was apparently able to do anything."*

Violet gave out a soft cry, not of pain but of wonderment.

"Oh my! Flowers and all," she half laughed.

Now before them was a set of descending stone steps, the bottom could not be seen.

"Do we dare?" she asked quietly.

"At this point, I think not."

Instant disappointment on Violet as she pleaded;

"But isn't this what we came here for?"

"Yes, I guess it was. But it is already past noon and we didn't bring lunch or even water. Do you think it's wise to go traipsing around to who knows where with out any sustenance?"

"Will this do."

She happily pulled out a few power bars from her waist pouch along with a small thermos of Whispering Wind's famous lemon drink.

"You truly are a wonder woman," Eric shot back.

Laughing now Violet asked again.

"Now can we go on?"

He could not help but laugh with her.

"Okay, you get to go first."

"I knew you would see it my way."

"Never mind that Pocahantas," Eric smiled as he patted her fanny as she passed by. "Now move."

She jokingly yelled "Spousal abuse."

Eric took notice of the direction they started off with, which was North by Northwest. He hoped he could keep track of any turns and which direction they went to basically keep track of where they were going. So far so good. There were a few turns, both right and left but the north by northwest direction basically held true.

Almost two hours passed with out a word spoken. Then suddenly faint voices were heard. Neither could make out what was being said but definitely a human voice.

Violet and Eric looked at each other with obvious questions on their minds yet not a word was spoken. They continued on and the voices, naturally became louder and closer though they still could not understand the words.

They stopped to discuss their options. To continue on

or turn back. The unknown sort of triggered their curiosity. The challenge to continue on but at a slower pace won out. They both laughed inwardly b y the fact that their curiosity won out over logical judgement.

The same mysterious lighting system was present which yet amazed them both. This truly was an advanced mind to have developed this long before what we call modern history.

They continued on but slowly and cautiously. They still could not understand the words they were hearing.

Another fifteen minutes and they were suddenly face to face with three men. Startled both parties were but neither frightened. Simultaneously the question was put forth.

"What are you doing here?"

There was laughter all around. The strangers, at least to Eric and Violet, spoke English quite well which confused them both. There confusion must have shown in their quizzical expressions.

"You are obviously from down state." said one of the strangers. "We, much to your obvious surprise, are natives of Alaska. And also obviously, the question on both our minds is what are you doing here."

The gentleman asking the question was a native Alaskan doing personal research and just happened to be an Archeological Scientist.

Eric quickly outlined his background.

"Oh so you're the one Carlos told me about,"

The surprise must have visibly shown on Eric's face because the next words he heard were

"Small world isn't it."

Eric's mind instantly went to work.

"What and who doesn't Carlos know in this world? And to think, when I first met him I thought he was just a native porter Frank had hired to carry baggage."

Violet was just quietly smiling during this whole exchange.

Eric finally continued;

"Getting back to our mutual question, what are you

doing here. And more importantly, why?"

"That's the easy question. By the way my name is Stanislous Ognashgut and don't ask about its history. Most people just call me Stan. Now to answer your question. Myself and a colleague accidently discovered a "Lost World" as you call it, in North Central Alaska. Right in the middle of the most desolate place on earth. Trust me it was purely by accident. We were really searching for lost Inuit villages. Our first look at it, was I guess, probably like yours. Just a thing of beauty to behold. Which in itself was a puzzle. Why this and why here? My next step of course was to contact Carlos. Based on our previous conversations this was more up his ally and yours from what I gather from Carlos. Before we go any further I wish not to ignore this lovely lady."

Turning to Violet he continued;

"And you must be the "Golden Lady, heir to the beauty of Nefertiti. And from what I am looking at it is all true.

Violet was flush with embarrassment nevertheless thanked the gentleman for his compliment.

Eric, internally proud, resumed the conversation.

"Not to be presumptuous but did Carlos discuss with you worm holes?"

A smile slowly crept across Stan's face.

"As a matter of fact the subject did come up. At first I thought he had lost his marbles. On further readings of Stephen Hawking I was beginning to understand where he was coming from. Hence why we are both here. We have walked about an hour and a half from our "Lost World". What about you?"

Eric looked at Violet who confirmed about two hours but at a slow walking pace.

There was a pause by all while Stan checked his note book.

"You said you came from the four corners area and we from central Alaska. That gives us a distance of plus or minus twenty six hundred miles. A distance which is absolutely impossible to walk in a few hours. Hence these Earth bound worm holes and not in a Black Hole in outer space."

He sort of snickered at what he just said and added;

"I don't know if I believe it myself and yet I'm living it."

Dove of Spring entered the discussion with;

"We also felt the same way when we traveled from Egypt to meet our colleagues from the Yucatan. That I believe was approximately seventy two hundred miles. You can't even fly that fast."

"Okay" said Stan as he directed his look to Eric.

"You're the expert. What do we do next?"

"Nothing, at least not yet. I'm sure you will agree that this needs a lot more study and by better people than us. We are now talking Quantum studies and that's out of my league. What we can hope to study is the why of it all."

"You are right. Finding these tunnels was almost the easy part. I'm with you there on the big question of why. I'm just a plain old Archeologist specializing in Alaska where I grew up."

Violet suggested we head back to reality. None of us objected. We said our farewells after exchanging contact information and started home.

Believe it or not I was actually looking forward to it.

We took up a slightly faster pace and before we knew it we were admiring the flowers again in our own "Lost World". I think I even detected a look of relief in Violet.

"Now what." I thought.

My queen must have been reading my mind.

"I really think both of us should just relax for the rest of the day and forget about other worlds. I have laundry to do and you can cut the grass."

She said all this while smiling her love.

I accepted my orders and headed for the lawn mower.

Chapter 9

Dove of Spring was correct in dismissing Other Worlds for a time. It allowed us to put our minds back together so to speak.

Another relaxing evening in the three tree jungle refreshed both mind and body.

The next morning the idea of Whispering Wind's hogan struck both of us at the same time. We were silent as we walked hand in hand to the museum. Violet even brought the lemon drink. After all being at Whispering Wind's Hogan without the lemon drink would be like a birthday cake without candles.

I was still impressed at the memorabilia this man had collected over his lifetime. A lifetime which no one really knew the length of. He was most likely older than his admitting years.

It was a quiet day which is what we really needed in order to do the research we came for.

I immediately went for the boxes of trade contracts, while Violet recovered the now personal writings of Whispering Wind. These were comparable to his personal history or his experiences with all he met.

It took a while for me to settle down to actual research. I was constantly drawn to the many priceless and ageless artifacts hanging on the walls or just standing around. I also remembered the hidden basement, if you will. I had not been down there yet. In all fairness though I would wait and do that with Dove of Spring.

I was still fascinated by all these tribal contracts. I knew they were old yet did not know their true age. I would have to wait for Dan or Violet to do some translation for me. My own meager knowledge did, however, allow me to identify the many different peoples the ancient Navajo were trading with.

Jade and turquoise appear to be the most desired items. Though maize and squash were also traded. The hand made rugs were not exactly unpopular either.

The other side of the trade agreements were also a mix of items. Pottery, I guess, being the most desired. Apparently the early Navajo had a fascination with the sea. Small model boats were also taken in trade even though there were no large bodies of water any where near here. Though who knows where the original home of the Navajo was. This and the other reservations were only recently occupied by comparison.

Eric continued to ponder this question as he sorted through these many hundreds of contracts covering many years. But again he would need help with the translations. He was quite content to review each one the best he could.

Violet on the other side of the hogan was in her glory sorting through many years of history. Apparently Whispering Wind was quite a history buff himself. He recorded many things and also had the presence of mind to secret them away for future study. This was part of his greatness, recording history.

Violet suddenly found what she did not know she was looking for. References to the "Golden Lady".

It appeared that she was given freely by whoever in trade for many buffalo hides and even a few horses. The year or years gone by were still a mystery. She was taken as a wife to one of the warriors and did bear some children.

The children remained with the Navajo nation but she traveled south with a group looking for better lands. Keeping with her, her Egyptian identification always. Hence a final arrival in the Yucatan. Obviously she remained there until her passing.

Here Violet set aside the papers and dwelled on what she just read. Talking to herself she smiled realizing her decision to stay with these new people.

From what little history she acquired from Mario and the other Mayan's she, now named the "Golden Lady" stayed and was accepted and loved for who she was as a person.

Violet knew she would have to follow up now with more history of the peoples of the Yucatan to further the story of this long lost relative.

As if on que they both put aside their papers and headed for the refreshing lemon drink. Laughing they both ran to be first. Violet was first but bowed and said;

" I wouldn't want to see you cry so you can help yourself first."

That's just what Eric did but he filled both cups and handed one to Violet.

"My Queen always comes first."

"Aren't you sweet. Just for that, I will make you a special supper tonight."

"That sounds fine to me but if you don't mind now I would like to go back to the contracts."

Violet nodded and immediately headed for Whispering Wind's journals.

As Eric reviewed in more detail the contracts before him his imaginative brain started working on its own again.

"These are more than contracts with Egyptians." He said aloud to himself. They also span hundreds if not thousands of years. I know it would take a long time to decipher all of these yet I'm sure it would prove me right."

He sorted through the mess in front of him and finally pulled one out. Again speaking out loud;

"This, as far as I can detect is definitely Old Norse. We already know the Vikings were here in North America a few hundred years before Columbus."

He rummaged through the pile again and found another questionable paper.

"I'm no expert but this to me says early Italian or

perhaps Roman, which ever doesn't matter. It proves contact long before the accepted paradigm.

Yeah, like whose going to believe me. Even with this living, breathing proof it would be like climbing Mount Everest bare foot."

Eric could feel the frustration setting in. He put aside the papers and focused on the antiques hanging around the hogan now museum. His time with Whispering Wind was much too short.

Where do I or we even start. Even with this concrete proof we are looking at a brick wall. Make that a solid rock wall, he joked to himself.

"I need a break, I guess I'll go and see what Violet is up to."

Eric sat beside his Dove of Spring and was there for quite a while before she even realized it. She was so wrapped up in her history she was unaware of his presence. As she reached for another of Whispering Wind's journals she startled herself because of Eric's presence beside her.

"Oh, you almost frightened me. You really move quietly don't you?"

"Too much time in the jungle I guess," was his smiling answer.

Violet suddenly let loose her excitement

"You are not going believe what I have found. Whispering Wind knew about my history all along., yet never said a word."

"Perhaps he felt you were not ready yet," put forth Eric.

"I know you are most likely correct but I still wish I had known this before."

"But would it have meant as much before you met the "Golden Lady," Eric answered.

"I hate it when you are always correct, but in a way I love you for being you. Now what about you? Have you made any progress with the trade contracts?"

"I certainly have. To me this is undisputable proof of

world contact. And I mean world wide contact. Whispering Wind was wise to keep these records as were the others before him. I sometimes wonder how we ever made it to where we are today. There has been so many doubts thrown up against any type of discovery by so called experts. I am not questioning their science or studies in their fields but in my own non-sophisticated way I feel most have stopped short in their thinking and closed the door on intrusive evidence that would upset their theories."

"**W**ow! You certainly have been doing some deep thinking," smiled Violet.

"**R**emember these are strictly my own thoughts. I'm sure the rest of the world does not agree with me," returned Eric.

Violet closed the journals and put them securely away.

"**C**ome on big guy. I think it's time we went home. I'll fix that special meal I promised for you and then we can both retire to our three tree jungle with our thick black syrupy coffee and Cognac, of course. And then when we are settled and calmed down we will discuss our future and the future of the world. I think I would like that."

Eric smiled knowing she was right, for now anyway, and that she was right for him.

Dinner, as promised, was superb and the aroma of the thick coffee was sure enough getting to Eric. He was actually looking forward to the nights discussion being more than willing to share these thoughts and ideas with his personal "Golden Lady"."

He saw to the Cognac while Violet brought the coffee to their private jungle. In fact, anticipating a long evening he carried out the bottle and carefully placed it where it could not be knocked over.

Violet inwardly smiled at his acceptance of her planned evening.

Slowly sipping their coffee they remained silent, each unwinding in their own way. The moon was a day or so shy of a full moon and the scent of the fresh cut grass was the perfect touch to the twilight settled in semi darkness. They remained hushed for quite a while just enjoying the restful peace and listening to the noise of the night. Not quite like the real jungle but stress reducing just the same.

Without being asked Eric filled both snifters with his favorite drink. Violet took the offered glass with a loving smile murmuring

"The perfect start to our evening. Okay, now my "Chosen One," what has got you so down about the crazy world we live in?"

"That's just it. You hit it on the head. This crazy world we live in. I'm trying to convince myself that the Lost Civilization had solved such problems and lived in harmony with each other."

"Do you think that's possible?" inquired Violet.

Pondering for a moment, he finally answered in a very positive tone.

"Yes, believe it or not, I do. We must first get rid of the ME thinking, and yes I think that is also possible."

Looking directly at him she agreed.

"Wouldn't that be a wonderful thing. You are right. It most likely is possible. But with the world the way it is, It certainly will not happen overnight."

Eric laughed along with her words.

"Perhaps it will take two overnights."

Dove of Spring turned serious again.

"Let's get back to the "Lost Worlds" again. You appear to be unsettled by them of late. Is there a reason why?"

"Perceptive woman" he thought.

"Actually you are correct in that diagnosis. I am out of sorts lately by these many "Lost Worlds" which lead me to believe there are others. How many? Who knows? It's the why of it that has me totally befuddled."

"Do you have in mind where else we may find a "Lost World?"

"No, not exactly. It's just a gut feel, but I'm sure there are others. It stands to reason that there are others. Yet again

I don't know the why of it. That is what really has me stumped. I can understand a lost advanced civilization. Most likely more advanced than we are, otherwise they would not have the things we are only now discovering."

"If you don't mind me asking, what brings you to that conclusion?"

Smiling now and with a sip of Cognac Eric slowly answered.

"This Quantum world we are now entering. These earth bound worm holes, when we are only now encountering them in outer space. I'm sure Stephen Hawking and Albert Einstein would have loved to have seen these let alone figure out why and how they work."

Dove of Spring was lingering on Eric's every word. It was easy to follow his thinking but it never crossed her mind to think along those lines.

"I'm going to forget about a second Cognac so that I can clearly continue to follow along." she thought to herself.

Violet was more and more interested in what Teller of Stories was presenting.

"If you don't mind me asking, where do you think this is all going to lead us."

"That's easy," answered Eric. "TROUBLE" with a capital "T".

Violet was a bit taken aback with his answer. She did not quite understand his answer and was surprised by it.

"Why would you think such advancements would cause trouble?"

Eric smiled.

"Look at us. Look at us as a whole world. We are controlled by a greedy, power hungry domineering few. And they take advantage of every moment just for continued control. Yet I honestly believe the majority do not think this way. They truly want peace and cooperation. Not just with their neighbors but with the world. But because most people want peace and to be left alone it is very easy for the few to control the many."

"**N**ow that you put it that way, I cannot disagree with you. The big question is how do we solve this world wide problem. We are only a handfull of people.

"**R**ight you are my queen. How?"

They were both silent. Their silence remained as they listened to the sounds of the night.

"**O**h if the world could only pay attention to the creatures of nature, imagine the peace we could attain.

Violet knew she had to get her man out of the world disturbances funk. But how?

"**P**erhaps we should forget about this Lost World stuff for now and concentrate on the more positive aspects of our recent adventures and I don't mean just the last few weeks. I'm thinking about the last few years. The Yucatan, the people who still wanted the "Golden Lady", the protection of the new discoveries of the old ways. This should be brought to the attention of the whole world. This, if approached in the proper manner could instigate some serious thinking about our past and its connection to our future."

"**P**hew! I haven't said that much since my university days" offered Violet to help lighten the moment."

"**Y**ou're right, I guess I am getting a little carried away," offered Eric. " I'm sorry, but you asked. I'm glad you did. I think I can now look at this whole thing from a different perspective. And hopefully from a better view."

Violet was glad to hear such words. She more than anything wanted to see him relax and look at things from a different point of view that would not tear him up inside.

"**O**kay, now my Chosen One, what say we contact your friends of the Maya people and discuss this and add their point of view."

"**I** guess that's why I love you. You know just how to calm me down."

"**G**ood, I'll take a second Cognac now," as she offered her glass.

"**A** wise woman she is," thought Eric as he refilled both their glasses.

"**I** think that's a wonder full idea, and first thing

tomorrow we will see about contacting them."

The tomorrow came and Eric was true to his word. He did manage to contact Mario at their Arizona University.

A tentative date was established to meet.

Teller of Stories and Dove of Spring. would go to Arizona.

This would allow the others not to disturb their classes. It would be a few more months before the jungle would allow research.

It was then set that Eric and Violet would again travel to the Yucatan. A face to face meeting by all, knowing something concrete would result.

This introduction of Worm Holes, to what was thought of as advanced peoples surely set us back to serious thinking. We, as a people are not really as advanced as we think we are.

Both Violet and Dove of Spring were looking forward to the end of the rainy season.

Dove of Spring in particular anticipated another visit to the people who knew her as their Queen.

She did not view this as deceiving these humble people, but actually viewed this as an advancement for the future. To believe in some idea, or some one, was important for future growth. Future growth as a people or future growth to equal their ancestral heritage.

She knew she had many months to prepare and would plan accordingly. She hoped to truly leave some sort of message with these real citizens of the world, and in particular their civilization. To give them a future to look forward to, not by changing them or their ways but to give them hope for their own Mayan future.

Their past was so glorious why shouldn't the future be the same, as knowledgeable leaders of the world.

*"**C**ome back to earth Violet."* she scolded herself internally. *"You still have many months to plan. Think of the lost Mayans, not yourself."*

She laughed at herself and her own thoughts.

"They may seem backwards to some but I would wager they are a lot happier as a whole."

She smiled inwardly and turned her attention back to Eric.

"Have a nice vacation my love?" he asked with a smile. The two of us make a good pair. We both live in two different worlds at the same time, or is it three?"

Dove of Spring then explained her thoughts of the "Golden Lady" visiting the ancient Mayan village again and the reason why.

Eric was in total agreement and ventured a guess that the others would be also.

"What's your choice now my Queen. Do we continue here on research or would you care for a short ride to the pet store for some Mr. Blue treats.?"

With this her eyes lit up.

"Yes let's do that. I do hope he's still around. We have been gone for a while."

"I hope so also, so let's go and find out for sure."

In less then an hour the pair were standing in front of the desert pyramid. Eric mentioned that Dan's teens were doing an excellent job in maintaining the historic structure.

"I'll have to remember to tell Dan and his teens. I'm proud of them."

They only had to wait around five or six minutes when sure enough out came Mr. Blue. Eric was about to open the bag of treats when Mr. Blue by passed him heading straight for Violet. Stopping about three feet from her and made a motion unfamiliar to Eric. Violet noticed the different move also.

"If I didn't know better I would say he just bowed to you."

"I would agree with you on that. I know this will sound silly, but I actually had a strange internal feeling when he did that. I really do think he was bowing, not to me but to Nefertiti."

"After what we have been through these last few years

with receiving telepathic messages from long past guardians, it probably was a sign of respect. Well, I guess Mr. Blue belongs to both of us now."

Eric's statement filled Violet with an additional sense of pride. So much so that she blushed. She turned away from Eric but not soon enough.

"You should be proud my love. Don't ever be ashamed of a connection to nature's others creatures."

As if nothing happened Eric knelt down and spilled the bag of treats on the ground which Mr. Blue made short work of.

Eric looked at the pyramid area again, his mind drifted away as usual.

"Why am I so captivated by the unknown. Finding this pyramid was like finding my life all over again. I have the same internal revelations that first were in the jungle. I could feel my life changing. From the mundane and routine to new knowledge and the desire to seek and learn more. To what end I knew not but the excitement of discovery and learning fueled my imagination."

Looking back to my life in Vermont was really eye opening. I, at the time, appeared to be happy in my routine, the mundane life of just taking pictures that made others happy. But was I? Who knows? I thought I was. Then I got that phone call from Frank Thurber asking if I was interested in plying my craft in the jungles of the Yucatan. He needed honest and real documentation of his discovery of a new lost city of the Maya. Who knew all this would lead me to where I am today. Which is in a life no longer mundane but filled with new excitement every day.

If today's world would only pay attention to the past, I believe we would actually learn more than we think we know. I do believe "Lost Civilizations" did exist and were trying to pass along their wisdom. We just refused to listen.

Now here I am today caught in the middle of the two worlds. What's even more strange is the fact that I like it.

A soft gentle touch brought me out of my reverie.

"I believe Mr. Blue was trying to thank you but you were some place else."

I looked around but Mr. Blue had already departed.

Finally grabbing hold of myself I looked at my wife. Yes my wife. Not Violet or Dove of Spring or the "Golden Lady" and not even Nefertiti. My wife. The real one who keeps me on the straight and narrow. The one who keeps me grounded.

I think she even knows what I was thinking right now.

She reached out and took my hand, grasping tightly and without words said we are one. No matter what each of us do, we do as one.

I suddenly felt better. Alive again and ready to pursue my, or should I say, our future, no matter what it may be. A real future of something involving a "Lost Civilization".

Our past is the future and our future is our past. All we have to do now is convince the rest of the world.

I, now , was a whole new man.

Chapter 10

Back in the real world again Eric looked at Violet but knew he did not have to apologize for drifting yet again. He took her hand and they walked closer to the pyramid.

"Impressive structure isn't it?" he put forth. "Talk about your Egyptian connection, this sort of solidifies the truth of it."

"Perhaps to you and me and a few others but what about the rest of the doubting world," Violet answered. "Not only the Egyptian connection but we must not leave out the Mayan connection, or those before the Mayans."

"Very astute young lady. That is something we, or at least I , failed to do while in Egypt."

"We can always go back." smiled Violet.

"Perhaps so, but not just yet. I haven't caught up with all the first time changes yet. Let's say we just stay put for a little while longer. By the way, in your readings of the journals of Whispering Wind, did you come across any mixing of the Maya and Egyptian peoples?"

"Not yet but I have an inner feeling that he has other writings secreted away somewhere. What about you? Does anything stand out in the trade contracts?"

"Funny you should ask. There are a lot more to go through yet, but their appears there was also many trade agreements with China."

"I didn't want to hear that." she answered. "I'm confused enough as it is now."

There was a short pause as they both laughed. Then

Eric suggested

"Let's get more confused together in the pyramid. Who knows we may have missed something on our other visits."

Dove of Spring was amenable to this.

We entered the pyramid and again I was amazed. Everything was neat and cleaned and orderly. Dan's teens were doing one hell of a job in maintaining this piece of history. It's good to see such loving care for a thing of history. This wasn't just their history but actually world's history. This small hiccup belongs in the book of the peoples history. Violet looked on with pride also. Proud of her people.

We rode down in the elevator, the newly strengthened elevator. It was now a safe ride down.

We wandered around all the familiar places yet there appeared nothing new or even a hint of something to investigate. Then out of the blue Violet commented

"Eric, if you don't mind me putting my two cents in, I would like to make a suggestion."

"Go right ahead my Queen, this is your homeland."

"Well, to date everything you and Dan have discovered here has always been down, hidden underground, or under floors."

"Yes, so what's your point?"

"Well, my point is the pyramids in Egypt were built with tunnels, passageways and rooms going up. All above the floor ground level. Small upward tunnels aligned with certain stars or constellations. Have you ever checked anything going up?"

"It looks like you have done it again. After finding all that interesting stuff hidden underground, the thought never occurred to us to look up."

Then as if a light bulb went on in his head he quickly blurted out; "We never looked up in the Yucatan either."

Then smiling he added, "The only time we really looked up was to yell at the Howler monkey's."

They both laughed at this.

"And deservedly so." added Violet.

"Looks like we could use Dan on this one."

"Why Dan?" quizzed Violet.

"He's the one with all the star charts. We would need a compass also. If this was built anything like the ones in Egypt, they have a definite geographical alignment. Dan's star charts will tell us what star or constellation we should be looking at."

"Well, since we do not have Dan at the moment we could still at least look." Violet smiled.

"You know just how to get to me, don't you?" smiling along Eric stated. "We might as well start where we found the book."

They proceeded to that area and began inspecting the walls going up. They both agreed they did not know what they were looking for, but occupied themselves with serious eye scans and careful touch and feel. The silence was almost scary.

Close to an hour went by with no results. With an unspoken agreement they rested.

Violet glanced at Eric who was slumped to the floor, his back against a wall for support.

"Careful, my love, it looks like a spider just above your head.

Eric quickly moved away from the wall while Violet moved towards him.

"Wait." she cautioned. "That's no spider, just some scratch marks on the wall.."

They both took a closer look. They were not just scratch marks, there was a design to it.

Eric softly spoke as if talking to himself.

"If I didn't know better I would say that looks like a star grouping."

On closer inspection Violet agreed. Neither was familiar with the grouping.

"Now I understand why you mentioned Dan." Violet remarked with her only as she can smile. "Should we wait for Dan or do you feel inquisitive enough to try the finger approach that you are so successful with?"

"You really do know me well, don't you."

Violet just answered with her winning smile.

His own curiosity now peaked Eric looked closer at the markings and realized they truly were some sort of scratch marks. Nevertheless he did go through the motions of the finger touch. He could only feel no indication or change of surface. They were truly scratch marks. He relayed his findings to Violet which was disappointing to say the least and she directed one of her favorite expressions to Eric.

"Party Pooper." Of course said with w smile.

"Now that we are finished with the highly technical stuff, what say you, we continue our leisurely walk while looking up."

"Lead on oh "Chosen One" she laughed.

They took their time doing what they thought was a thorough search. Their first place was the Turquoise room. Eric instantly remembered finding the two Mayan's they found here and the funeral service that was held.

Violet knew he was reflecting on that incident and let him have his precious moments.

Eric did not dwell on this for long and rejoined Dove of Spring in the search upwards.

They were just about to call it a day when Violet called out.

"Eric, come here, look at this."

He quickly joined her as she pointed.

"That darker spot. That stone block does not seem to match the others exactly. It appears to be cut more exactly to fit its space."

On closer inspection Eric agreed. The seam between blocks were more precise. The color was pretty much the same yet he did detect a slight mismatch. He stared at the spot for quite a while almost daring not to touch it. Yet internally arguing with himself. He knew this is what we were here for.

Violet remained silent.

Eric finally reached up towards the mismatch. Violet smiled to herself.

Ever so gently Eric first touched, then pushed. Almost without sound a small section did open showing a roughly six by six inch shaft going upwards. He stepped closer to center himself on the hole. True enough he could see blue sky above.

He stepped aside and silently indicated for Violet to look also. She was all smiles now and was actually thrilled at seeing the blue above.

Excitedly she wondered aloud

"I wonder if this aligns with the Orion Constellation?"

After a short hesitation Eric answered.

"I honestly don't think it will." Then quickly added, "I wish Dan were here."

He continued his thoughts out loud.

"This structure may have been built in the style of those in Egypt but in this western hemisphere the Orion position would be different and since we have a Maya - Navajo connection I would be willing to bet this would be aligned with the planet Venus. We should also check out the alignment of the kings tomb. I would say it would be exactly the same as this.

Venus was all important to the Maya. They have committed much study to the movement and position of this star planet. It was almost like a worship thing. They even had a special calender they called the Venus calender. It actually marked the planets movement on its yearly cycle as it traveled from the morning star to the evening star. Venus was all important ti their lives."

" Dan and his star charts should be able to clarify this for us. And I just remembered that Whispering Wind had a special fondness for Venus. He often mentioned to me how he tracked its movements across the heavens.

Violet moved to him and kissed his cheek.

"Boy, you sure learned a lot for only a few months in the Yucatan. Let's come back tonight and with Dan if possible."

"You took the words right out of my mouth," Eric smiled.

Hand in hand they headed for the car.

The drive back home was a happy one. They both were excited about the discovery and were looking forward to sharing it with Lone Buffalo.

Once home Violet went to fix some lunch, late though it was, while Eric headed straight for Dan's classroom.

Dan did not mind the interruption once he knew the reason, and yes he could make it tonight.

Eric told Violet of Dan's excitement so they prepared for the nights outing. They ate their lunch and decided to rest. Eric, in the recliner was fast asleep in minutes, while Violet had the foresight to set an alarm just in case.

~ ~ ~ ~ ~ ~

More than on time, Dan was a little early. His friends were just finishing up a snack. Equipped with his star charts and compass Dan was raring to go.

It was dusk when the trio finally headed for the pyramid equipped with hand carried lights and electric torches.. An obviously clear night was in their favor.

On the drive to the pyramid Dan explained his preliminary work for the nights viewing.

"There is the outside chance that we will not see Venus tonight."

Violet instantly took on a pout of disappointment.

Dan went on to further explain his statement.

"Yes, we are in the right part of the world yet not with a direct view of Venus as the Mayans have. I did some preliminary figures and there is some plus or minus twenty three hundred miles difference between us and the Yucatan. That alone changes the angle of direct viewing. So I can't promise an actual viewing of Venus tonight. Once we get there I will check the geographical alignment of the structure and then we can compare it to both Egypt and the Yucatan pyramids. I would also be interested in that other pyramid when we took our Queen to visit. For some reason or another I have a feeling there are many secrets yet to be discovered in that building.

But getting past the head honcho there I suspect is going to be quite difficult."

"**P**erhaps the "Golden Lady" can help along those lines,“ smiled Dove of Spring.

Smiling in return Eric politely questioned;

"**Y**ou really are anxious to go back there aren't you?"

"**T**o be perfectly honest, yes I am. Those children really captured my heart."

"**O**kay then, tomorrow I will contact Mario and find out when they are headed back there.

"**O**h goody," spouted Violet as a little child would do.

Both Dan and Eric agreed there would be no controlling her now.

Finally at their destination the three could not wait to get to the viewing tunnel. They could already see stars appearing on this perfectly clear night.

First things first. Dan took some compass readings of all four sides for plotting as accurately as he could.

Once inside they went directly to the turquoise room.

Mr. Blue was waiting right under the viewing spot. He appeared happy to see them but did move to a far corner and proceeded to munch on one of his treats while watching everyone.

"**H**ow does he do that?" asked Dan out loud.

"**D**o what?"

"**K**now exactly what we are going to do before we do."

Dan, star chart in hand was the first to look upwards. His head moved back and forth from the viewing tunnel to his chart. He did this for a solid five minutes before speaking.

"It's in its waning phase but it is Venus."

"**W**hat do you mean waning phase?" Violet asked.

"**I**t is changing from it's position as the evening star to the morning star which does take months, but it is definitely Venus."

Eric and Violet each took turns gazing up at this latest discovery. Violet, of course was absolutely thrilled with this discovery of the night.

Dan went on to further explain how important Venus was to the Maya and perhaps even those before them. So much so that they even had a calendar based on the movements of Venus both as a morning and evening star.

Violet was more and more involved in this intrigue of the "Lost Civilization" that so few even knew about including herself until a few short years ago. Now here she was not only learning about it but actually a part of it. Her being a descendent of the one and only Nefertiti was the thrill of her lifetime. She knew then the rest of her life would be pursuing this Lost Civilization.

And to think, she thought to herself, *of the original doubts she harbored about Eric and his wild stories.*

~ ~ ~ ~ ~ ~

The three returned home with Dan saying goodnight. This of course left Eric and Violet to relax in the three tree jungle with of course their favorite Cognac.

"**D**o you really believe these tunnels or worm holes are the real thing?" questioned Violet softly.

Eric, with a slight smile was not surprised by her question. He sometimes had doubts himself.

"**A**ctually I do. I did have my own doubts earlier, but this is too unbelievable not to be true. It has finally settled firmly in my mind that we are dealing with a very, very advanced people. We are only now discovering these so called Worm Holes hidden in outer space connected with the Black Holes of the universe. These people some how perfected them to the point of using them here or rather in this planet. What happened to them? We will most likely never know. Obviously something catastrophic occurred wiping out a knowledge we are only now realizing existed. We, as a people, have a lot of catching up to do. What we few, you and I and our Maya friends and I'm sure a few others, have discovered purely accidentally, is just the tip of the iceberg as they say."

Eric then laughed at what he had just said.

Violet's confusion must have shown on her face for Eric then explained his sudden laugh.

"The last ice age some twelve thousand plus or minus years ago could have been the culprit that triggered the destruction of that brilliant civilization. I even wonder if they were advanced enough to have left this planet and settled elsewhere."

"And that is something we will never know." joined Violet. "We are the neophytes when it comes to space exploration. We still consider the "Hot Dog" a culinary advancement," she added laughing.

This little drift from seriousness was just what Eric needed to restart his mind. *"Enjoy the night, the Cognac and most of* all *your wife,"* he silently scolded.

He right away changed the subject somewhat.

"I know we have a lot of research to do before we return to the Yucatan but putting that aside for now, what are your plans for a visit to the ancient village and the children?"

The face of Dove of Spring came alive instantly with Eric's question.

"You are correct, I am genuinely looking forward to that visit."

"Do you plan anything special or just a hello, how are you doing?"

Violet grinned at Eric's little pun but did answer right away.

"I was hoping to introduce a little game to them to further their happy life."

"I'm glad you recognize their life and do not want to change it as so many outsiders are attempting to do. Most of these ancient peoples probably lead a slower, happier lifestyle than the so called modern world we are part of."

Eric said this almost sarcastically. Violet knew exactly what he meant and did not disagree.

Chapter 11

True to his word, the first thing Eric did the following day was to contact Mario.

A final date was not quite set due to the unpredictable weather but it was narrowed down to within a week or two. This gave Violet and he more than enough time for planning and tying up loose ends; mainly more research on the "Lost Worlds" and on a personal note more and thorough study on the worm holes.

Violet assured Eric she also wanted to be part of that study. She felt her background in engineering would be helpful. She was not unfamiliar with the subject of Quantum Mechanics. Admittedly it was deeper than her actual studies yet she was always open to new research.

After a comforting breakfast Eric and his Queen planned a day at the library to do what ever reading they could on Quantum Mechanics. As luck would have it there were a few books by Stephen Hawking and also a few about him and his theories.

Finding a secluded corner the couple sat quietly devouring all they could and taking notes accordingly. Not a word was spoken for well over two hours.

Eric was the first to give in to his hunger spasms. He also felt some mild eye strain.

Violet noticed his movement and joined him back in the real world.

"Wow!" she said. "I feel like I'm back in college."

"I can understand that. I suggest we call it a day due

to brain overload," stated Eric.

Violet chuckled at his remark but also agreed.

"**W**hat now? Oh master of the universe?" joked Violet

Smiling in answer Eric responded,

"**A** light lunch at Whispering Wind's museum and more record research."

"**G**ood," responded Dove of Spring. "I'll make sure we have plenty of lemon drink."

Of course Eric smiled at this.

~ ~ ~

Comfortably seated at the hogan museum each silently continued the record checking. Violet with Whispering Winds diaries or journals and Eric again sorting through trade agreements.

Shockingly Violet came across some notes referencing some visits of people from the west. People unlike themselves yet again not like European either. After reading further descriptions she surmised these visitors were Chinese. It was a known fact that China had an advanced Navy and did some extensive travel southward along the coast of both North and South America. Who knows how far beyond that.

She paused here just staring blindly at the journals.

*"**T**his world of the past was far more advanced than today's experts want to give credit for. Why, as a people of today, are we so close minded about the past."*

Here Violet laughed at herself.

*"**N**ow I'm starting to sound like Eric."*

She rested her eyes while serving herself some refreshing lemon drink. Gazing over to where Eric was seated she saw that he was in one of his far away worlds again.

*"**I** wonder where he is this time?"* she thought but decided

to let him be. He will join the living again soon," she chuckled.

Eric, truly was in another world at this time. Reading through these trade agreements triggered his mind back to the King's tomb in the Yucatan and the Egyptian connection.

"Why is today's world so close minded about the past. There have been so much positive evidence contrary to the paradigm thinking. Only a few of today's scholars are recognizing the advanced scholarship of the ancient Maya with their calendar and mathematics and astronomy. We could actually learn from them. Who knows how much was destroyed by the conquering Spanish, who burned books and writings of knowledge of the universe, sun and planets, Venus and the Sun being a concentrated focus. They, I'm beginning to believe, are or were part of the "Lost Civilization." The lost knowledge we are only now discovering and will probably take us several lifetimes more before we catch up to their advanced why of the world."

After thinking this way the more I want to go back to the Yucatan and grounding myself. To go back and find the real truth of things. Violet can have her time with the children, I want my time with history. The history that no wants to admit to. The story of the real "Lost World"

"The one before us. The one that is the real advancement of knowledge. The one that we are deceiving ourselves about. We should be learning from the past, yet we seem not to want to do that. What made us so brilliant that we have become stupid and non accepting."

Eric took a few deep breaths and cautioned himself.

"Slow down boy. You are going to give yourself a stroke with all this worry that you have no control over. Remember your own words to Dove of Spring. We can only control ourselves. The rest is out of our hands.

Eric took a few deep breaths to control himself and calm down.

"Thank you Violet for keeping me grounded." he said silently to himself. "Without you, under these circumstances who knows where I would end up."

Taking a few more deep breaths Eric tried to ground himself.

"Come back to reality," he urged.

There was a short pause when Eric allowed his mind to go blank.

He finally came out of his trance to see a concerned Violet next to him actually holding his hand.

The first thing he did was to apologize. For obviously upsetting her. He now knew how to control his mind and promised not to get carried away again in the worlds future and past. He would seek her council on all matters from now on.

She held him close and repeated his own words. From here on they would always share their thoughts no matter negative or positive they were. They were to become as one.

I should have been embarrassed by my previous actions but for some reason I wasn't. I didn't even apologize to Dove of Spring. Instead I took on a positive attitude. I openly relayed to her how anxious I was to get back to the Yucatan.

She was all smiles at hearing this.

"But first," I said with a smile, "We both still have a lot of studying to do. And I mean we. I want to read more Hawking, and I believe you want to prepare for your children's visit. So let's get to work right now."

Violet's reaction took me by surprise. She kissed me and pulled me by the hand towards the door saying,

"Then let's get to work right now."

Laughing now Eric emphasized, "Whoa, slow down girl. Don't you think we should put away these books and papers first?"

Now laughing at herself Violet answered, "Of course, I don't know what I was thinking."

They proceeded to clear away their books and papers and anxiously , hand in hand headed home, still not able to make the pace that Whispering Wind always set.

Once home Eric buried himself in the Hawking and other related books while Dove of Spring was deeply involved in the appropriate Queens attire and designing a game for the children.

Dan was naturally invited to participate and did so when time permitted. In addition to that he was working on plans for his teens so that he could also return to the jungle. He looked forward to that revisit.

Time appeared to drag on slowly yet at the same time was going too fast. Eric wanted to do more research into the Quantum theories as did Dan for more study of the Venus history. On the other hand Violet decided on the game of Hop Scotch. It would allow for both boy and girl to participate equally. Working diligently she also designed attire befitting the Queens status without going overboard. It set her aside from other women yet blended at the same time. She was thankful her powers of observation were as sharp as they were.

The following many uneventful days were just that. Silent reading and note taking. Even the ever enthusiastic Eric was growing tired of the reading.

Mid morning one day he, out of the blue, told Violet to get ready. They were going to the pyramid. Surprised as she was, she did not object. She quickly grabbed some power bars and a thermos of lemon drink and was on her way to the car before Eric.

Smiling, he quickly followed and they were on their way before a word was even spoken. Finally Violet broke the ice.

"Why the sudden change of heart?"

Eric casually answered. "My head was getting too full of unbelievable things. Most likely all true but I needed to settle my brain or at least what's left of it. I seem to be able to think better at the pyramid."

"You miss the King's tomb, don't you?" she asked quietly smiling.

"Is it that obvious?" he asked.

"Yes, and I feel exactly the same way. I almost feel at

home there. The jungle is like a magnet. It keeps calling me back."

"That's because you have become a Chosen One whether you like it or not. You are a true Queen of the jungle. And lucky for me you are my Queen."

When they finally reached their destination they viewed an unexpected surprise. Dan and his teens were there doing their monthly cleanup, not that many people visited but the desert wind blown sand never left their cleanup alone. It really wasn't that much work and the teens always looked forward to a day away from the classroom. Additional knowledge and experiences never hurt anyone.

I thanked the young ones and complimented them on a job well done as did Dove of Spring. Her words meant more to them considering she was a tribal elder.

"Okay, now that we are here, why are we here?" asked Violet with a grin.

" I really don't know myself. I just find it more comfortable to think. I know you are next going to ask, to think about what. That, again I do not even know myself."

Drifting aimlessly they finally ended up at the turquoise room.

"This is where you found the book of our lost history," Violet stated matter of fact.

Yes it is and I think it is as good a place to start."

"To start what?" quizzed Violet instantly.

"To start looking for more answers about these world wide connections. Especially the why and how of them."

"Are you thinking you will find your answer here?"

"Just a gut feel. Why should there be Egyptians here among the Navajo, and why the Navajo and Egyptian in the Yucatan. What brought that about? What is the common denominator?"

Violet appeared slightly befuddled with Eric's words and let her mind run with them. They were both hushed now listening to the noise of nothing.

Silence remained for a spell. Not even breathing was

heard. Dove of Spring at last spoke softly as if still in a thinking mode.

"**A** quest for knowledge, a common knowledge."

"**E**xactly," returned Eric. "But how did they know to travel to find this common knowledge. What has been mans quest and fascination since the beginning of time."

Smiling broadly now Violet answered positively.

"**T**he heavens, the stars and the universe."

"**P**recisely! Every culture today is still fascinated by the sky's show. Except today we do it for scientific knowledge. A knowledge they already possessed. I would venture to guess cultures of our past did it for reasons of life. This sun, the moon, the skies, the universe itself has a meaning for life itself. All previous civilizations relied on these things. It ruled their lives. It was like a religion to them. Actually it was their religion and still is today to some. There I go again, getting carried away. I'm sorry."

"**D**on't be. I love it when you get into your teaching mode. I'm always up to learning new things. Please go on with your theory of why these connections."

"**W**ell, it has already been proven that trans Atlantic crossings have been made long before Columbus. Otherwise why would there be so many similarities in thinking, in construction, in mathematics and in Astronomy. The Maya, it has been shown, were way ahead of the rest of the world in Astronomy. Their many calendars prove that. Their Venus, almost worship like, was an eye opener to other so called advanced cultures. Their mathematics also was far ahead of many other peoples. Yet the first European adventurers thought they were ignorant and backwards by comparison. I think it was the Europeans of the time who were ignorant."

Eric paused here to calm himself down. Violet took his hand lovingly. Smiling she looked deep into his eyes and asked.

"**W**hat would you like for dinner tonight?"

Eric immediately started laughing.

"**T**his is why I need you. You know just how to settle me down. Now to answer your question. How about those advanced culinary delights you mentioned earlier?"

Violet seemed a bit confused.

Eric furthered, "You know, some Hot Dogs."

Now she really laughed.

With a total change of mood and heart, Eric now smiling positively stated,

"Let's go home now. There is nothing more for us here. The further answers we want are back in the Yucatan. I'm sure of it now."

"How can you be so sure of it now? We have already been half way around the world and have experienced three different "Lost Worlds."

"Yes, and all with more questions but no answers. Let's just say it's an internal feeling. The answers are back in the land of the Maya."

"Do you think you will find the whole answer?'

"Yes, I do." he answered confidently. "It may take a while but I think the answer is there. At least the answer to satisfy me."

"Oh Goody." Doing her child's answer again. "That way we can spend more time in the real jungle."

"Now you are starting to sound like Jane."

"Yes." she smiled in answer. "And you are my Tarzan. Let's go have some Hot Dogs," she laughed.

Chapter 12

The next few weeks dragged on slowly. At least it seemed that way to the three anxious researchers, though they did not consider themselves that.

Eric wanted to get to the truth of the Maya Egyptian connection. Violet wanted to return to the children, not to convert or change them but to encourage them to pursue their destiny.

Dan was truly just looking for the excitement of adventure. He had already found the right replacement to continue with his teens with the emphasis on both cultures, the Maya and Navajo.

The three knew not what was in store for them but the call and pull of the Yucatan was strong. They yearned for the unknown ahead of them.

Further readings of Whispering Wind's journals captured Violet's attention with the mention of Atlantis. Atlantis and Egypt, both were mentioned together and more than once. She brought this to Eric's attention immediately.

He appeared speechless at hearing this. He remained unmoving, his mind going in all directions. The name Atal spilled from his lips unconsciously.

"Atal - Atlantis" "Of course, now it is starting to make sense."

"What is?" inquired Violet.

"The connection." said Eric rather loudly.

"Calm down, my love. I'm right here next to you."

Eric sheepishly apologized yet continued excitedly but somewhat hushed.

At the soft touch of Dove of Spring Eric calmed down instantly.

He then related to her one of his very early conversations with Atal who he also referred to as the King. How he spoke of his home having met a disastrous end and lost to the sea. This was when he and others called the "Chosen Ones" set out for other lands to teach their much advanced knowledge which was not always accepted. The Egyptians and the people of the Yucatan were the only ones, although not all, who accepted and learned of this advanced wisdom. Hence the similarities of peoples thousands of miles apart. There must be hidden writings and records of this advanced wisdom in both places. It just has not been found yet."

Finished with his out loud thinking he smiled at Violet and giving her a loving hug and spoke a commanding order.

"Pack our bags. We are off to the Yucatan whether our Maya friends are ready or not."

This, of course, made Violet extremely happy and was heading for the exit of Whispering Winds hogan before Eric finished speaking.

"Whoa! Slow down girl. I didn't mean we were leaving this very second. I have some preparing to do first."

Violet stopped, turned around and with a half smile spoke her favorite accusation.

"Party Pooper."

Laughing now she returned to him with a big hug.

"I'm not quite ready myself, but I have been working on it."

She assisted Eric to tidy up the museum. They left together, hand in hand, as usual.

~~~~~~

The next few weeks were a whirlwind of activity. Packing was the least troublesome. It was more reading, note taking and study of the Sun, moon, Venus and star constellations.
~~~~~~

Lone Buffalo was honing his skills of the stars and planets for more accurate measurements of the pyramids structures in the Yucatan.

Dove of Spring was involved in careful examination of the pictures of the Golden Lady so that she could as accurately as possible duplicate her attire and overall look so she could become the Golden Lady, without the gold paint of course. She also remembered Diego's artistic talent and abilities of course and would count on his assistance to present a true Golden Lady or Queen.

Contact was maintained with the team at their Arizona College to best coordinate their travel timing.

Eric, Violet and Dan would be arriving first but would wait at the hotel at Oxaca for the others. This would then give them time to re-acclimate their bodies to the summer heat.

~ ~ ~ ~ ~ ~

Oxaca had not changed at all since Eric's first introduction years ago. He realized it would probably never change. He could understand this. Why change something that works and that everyone was happy with.

Colonel Ramirez was on hand to greet them and was genuinely pleased with their return. He reassured Eric all was well with the kings tomb and looking forward to the exchange of information again.

The three enjoyed the forced relaxation for three days although they were anxious to continue their research. They did however realize this forced relaxation was good for them. Both body and mind.

Mario and friends finally arrived and a grand celebration was had by all. This was apparently the busiest time ever for the hotel and they assisted in any and every way possible to make their welcome guests comfortable.

Porters were already on standby and the bark canoes

were on call at a moments notice. Besides the getting reacquainted party the next day was a serious review of the next step in planned activity. Eric withheld his opinion purposely until they were all settled at the home base of the kings pyramid. He was, however, very anxious to let his feelings be known because he did respect their input and would work accordingly.

Another fun and joyful day was spent getting together the necessary food and supplies and packing accordingly. At last all was set.

Colonel Ramirez said his good byes but assured us he would personally check on us at a future date.

Early the next morning they headed to the river where, as usual, the boatmen were already waiting. Eric smiled to himself recognizing the same ones as the last few years.

"It must be a quiet and peaceful life they lead." He thought. *"Obviously they did not have to worry about the rest of the world and its fast pace. Oh, to be that content."*

The trip to the first overnight stop was uneventful yet relaxing with the always beautiful jungle. Even Violet remarked that she never tired of its wonders.

They settled for the night with a quick meal, hung their hammocks and were fast asleep. Eric listened carefully to hear his jungle serenade and finally drifted to dreamland happy to be home again with his favorite real life music.

Up early and on their way with Violet pulling her fair share of the necessary baggage. As before a few porters were paid to help with the overload of baggage instead of them having to make two trips.

The king's tomb was a welcome sight. Some of nature's greenery again started to reclaim what she felt was hers, but overall things had not changed.

Before we even set up our camp the first thing was to pay homage to the King and of course Frank Thurber. Silence and respect was shown as a tradition of honor for Atl, the king. Eric was especially humbled before the king's final resting place. With extra care for Eric's sake Dove of Spring paid honor to the King's place of honor. She actually felt she was part of this heritage. Although she was Navajo and obviously Egyptian she felt a certain personal affinity to the Maya as if she were one of them.

Homage to the King having been humbly fulfilled they all turned to setting up their home base again. Even Violet proceeded to be very adept at setting up her own hammock. In fact she was finished before Eric much to his chagrin.

In truth Violet was beginning to feel at home here. *"Perhaps I am part Maya."* she told herself quietly. *"Enough of that silliness,"* she answered herself quickly and immediately sought out Diego.

As Eric and the others finished setting up their chosen sleeping areas they congregated at the kitchen and dining area. Having done this so often all was quickly in order with the thick syrupy coffee already brewing. Rest was now the order for the afternoon.

Coffee mugs in hand they one by one gathered at the main table. Carlos, as usual, took the lead.

"**I** understand our queen has plans for another visit with our ancient brethren. Perhaps she could enlighten us with a few details."

"**T**hank you kind sir, I would love to. Those children captured my heart completely. I thought I could spend more time with them. Not to change their life style, that would be totally the wrong thing to do. I just want to hopefully introduce more fun to their long days by introducing them to a simple children's game. Something for both boy and girl."

"**W**hat did you have in mind ?" asked Mateo.

"**H**opscotch. Which is a very simple game and also builds mind and body coordination. It is simple, easy and quick and can fill up some empty time. From what I saw on our last visit I think it would be welcomed."

Smiles went around the table and there were no dissenting remarks.

Violet hesitated a bit before continuing. She rather shyly offered an additional suggestion.

"I must admit I have an ulterior motive."

This caught the attention of all.

"On our last visit I had a short visit in their main structure with their apparent leader who appeared very secretive about his private domain. If you remember that's how I got the book. The book you all found so interesting."

Here she paused again.

"Don't leave us hanging." Mateo voiced anxiously.

Violet smiled and continued slowly.

"Well- - - - , I noticed when this haughty head man reached for the book it was among other books and scrolls. Actually quite a few. He was acting quite protective of them. My thought, at the time, was what was he trying to keep secret. These books might be of great importance to you and your research of your history and ancient civilization."

Here she hesitated again, not sure of what to say next. She finally decided to just say what was on her mind.

"Well - - - - I thought we might put our heads together and figure a way to gain access to them."

She smiled modestly and finished with,

"Okay, now I'll shut up."

Eric smiled to himself feeling quite proud of her. She was truly one of them.

Carlos, being the ever logical one was smiling while asking his next question.

"Do you think the Golden Queen can accomplish this and I don't mean just the children. Granted I have no doubt you can win them over."

Dove of Spring returning his smile now spoke with confidence.

"Yes Carlos. I do think we can manage this. If you gentlemen put your heads together, yes I do believe you can accomplish this. I know how important this is to your history."

"Do you yourself have any ideas on how to go about

this?"

Satisfied with her acceptance she smiled again.

"Not totally. I have been working on the queens attitude to further my acceptance and will work closely with Diego's artistic abilities to make me more convincing. I obviously will need a great deal of help with your language. Some I can hopefully learn but I will definitely need translation help. I'm sure we can work something out."

Here she stopped and looked directly into the eyes of Carlos. He was silent for a moment and finally broke eye contact and turned to the others.

"Well gentlemen, there you have it. The gauntlet has now been thrown down. Do we accept this lovely lady's challenge?"

"I don't think we have much choice," answered Mario. "We can not let her be one up on us again."

Of course he spoke these words with a smile looking directly at Violet.

"You truly are our queen," Diego furthered.

Coffee mugs were refilled and when all were settled again Eric called for their attention.

"I would like to draw your attention to the Lost Worlds. At least the ones we know of. And at the same time share my personal feelings about them."

"Sounds ominous" Carlos joined.

"Not really." answered Eric. But I have doubts and certain misgivings and I know Violet shares my concern."

Diego interrupted smiling.

"Wait one. I need another refill."

A few others joined him. When all were settled again the forever smile of Diego said,

"Okay, you can go ahead now."

Eric answered with an equal smile,

"Are you sure. I wouldn't want to inconvience you."

"That's quite alright . The stage is yours."

Eric then went on to explain about the Lost World they found in Egypt and of course the newly discovered tunnel or worm hole if you will.

" This as you all know lead them to meet the team from the Yucatan."

He furthered with the other worm hole from the Navajo reservation to Alaska.

"Yes, I heard about your surprise meeting with Stan." offered Carlos. "He called me the next day. He was as surprised as you were. Sorry for the interruption Go ahead with your point."

"Well - - - as of right now we know of four lost worlds as we call them. Who knows how many more there are that we don't know about. Not only that, but we have no idea who or what others know about them. To me it just stands to reason that there are others. Who and how many? Your guess is as good as mine."

Mario spoke up.

"So far we all know that and agree with what you are saying. Get to your point."

"That was part of my point. I for one want to keep this quiet. I don't think this information should go any further. At least until we know more about them ourselves."

"And your reasoning?" questioned Carlos in a serious tone.

"Well, you may not agree and perhaps I'm over thinking this but I'm a bit apprehensive. With the shape the world is in today this could lead to others making problems. Finding the Lost World parks is one thing but the tunnel discovery of active worm holes could lead to serious world problems, as if we didn't have enough already. Not everyone is for the advancement of peace. These worm holes, and chances are there are more, are a perfect tool for domination of the many by the few. I may be overwrought but I think this should remain our secret for now. Study for the advancement of science would be a good thing but it could easily go the wrong way. I personally don't think our world of today is ready for this technology, or for that matter even this hint of advanced technology. I personally think at this point in time we should keep this discovery to ourselves. There I've said my peace."

There was total silence.

Dove of Spring almost unnoticed reached for Eric's hand under the table and gave it a loving squeeze. Neither looked at the other. All eyes searched each others. Mateo was the first to speak.

"I for one am behind you one hundred percent. The very same thoughts have been plaguing me since our meeting in the hole a few months ago. This is almost too much for me to digest."

Mario joined in with, "My own thoughts exactly. I totally agree."

"Count me in." beamed Diego.

All eyes now turned to Dan and Carlos. Dan spoke first.

"I'm just a poor teacher but what Eric says makes sense to me."

Carlos was now in full smile.

"Once again we are in full agreement oh Chosen One. The King was right in his choice."

Eric was almost embarrassed but knew it was said with sincerity.

Carlos continued, "So for all we know the knowledge of these worm holes is limited to we few."

"And your friend in Alaska?" Eric asked.

"Oh yes I almost forgot. I will get in touch with him about our decision and don't think there will be any problem. We go back a long ways on many projects and I know he thinks pretty much like we do."

Eric felt a relief on hearing this.

"Okay! Now big guy, what do we do with these other world tunnels? Just ignore them?"

Mario directed his remarks to Eric.

"We quietly conduct further research on them to learn of the possibility of others. Perhaps this can be accomplished by a more detailed study of the two we know about. This would also require the assistance of your Eskimo friends. And of course, utmost secrecy."

This answer was obviously extremely logical and was agreed to by all.

The answer surprised all also because Dove of Spring was the one who spoke. Eric was a bit surprised himself but was extremely proud of his Queen. He finished her statement with,

"I could not have put it better myself."

All seven were looking at one another with all eyes going from face to face along with smiles.

After a long minute Carlos quietly broke the silence.

"Problem solved except for the logistics. In the meantime let us assist our Queen in her preparations for the upcoming visit to the children."

Smiles went around the table as eyes focused on Diego. Of course he knew they were referring to his artistic abilities yet still answered with,.

"Why is everybody looking at me?"

The impromptu meeting broke up each going their own way. Violet and Diego remained at the table discussing the presentation of the Golden Lady, without the gold of course. Eric wandered over to the working table and dove right into the air photos. This time he focused on the village of the ancient ones they would be visiting soon. After some preliminary viewing he signaled for Dan to join him.

"I would like you to confirm what I think I'm seeing. This particular series of aerial surveys was flown in a basic east west direction. I want you to look at this main structure and check the basic geographic alignment."

Never having any experience with stereo viewing of aerial photographs, Dan was amazed at what he could see. It took a while to do what was requested because of his fascination. However he did finally make some tracings that he could transfer to the Topo map Eric had in his hand.

"You are right Eric, this is the same basic alignment as our pyramid at the reservation. It is aligned with Venus. I would actually have to do the math due to the planet's oscillation over these hundreds of years but I'm certain it will prove out. And by the way I will finish my study of the King's pyramid but I'm sure your guess is correct, again aligned with Venus."

The next week was the usual research and recording of finds. What started as the one pyramid discovery years ago by Frank Thurber evolved into a large city complex spread out over many miles.

This ancient Maya settlement was now the hub of an obvious advanced peoples whose history goes back unknown years. The obvious Egyptian connection was a distinct eye opener. But the discovery of a Navajo connection really set accepted history on its ear. Convincing others of these indisputable facts was the major problem they now faced.

Eric now alone with his Aerial photo work again let his mind drift. In doing so he scolded himself.

"Forget about what the rest of the world thinks. You may never change that established mind set. You are here in the middle of a major world discovery with who knows what kind of outcome. Enjoy what you have here and learn from it. This advanced civilization has much to give. You and your friends are the lucky ones to benifit. Continue the search and all will work out."

He suddenly felt better. Smiling to himself now he said aloud, "You can't change the world but the world can change you. Accept the gift before you."

Mateo just happen to pass by,

"Did you say something? I really was not paying attention."

"Not really, Eric laughed "I was just mumbling to myself as usual."

Eric returned to studying his photos.

The second structure near the main pyramid at the ancient village caught his attention again. It appeared to be a low flat type pyramid similar to the one home to the "Golden lady". It appeared to also show similar alignment but some what displaced from the main structure.

He then moved to the master map to plot both structures. Eric was happy with his find. It was just as he thought. Without actually measuring distances, yet his familiarity with the Orion complex proved he was right. The King's tomb, the main pyramid and this new find were the same repeated distance and alignment as Egypt and other places that studied the stars. Of course that brought up another question. Why? What was this fascination with the Orion complex world wide? We are only now, in the twenty first century , putting together this knowledge of the Orion complex distances and measurements. Yet this was common knowledge a few thousand years ago. These mathematical relationships were used in many structures including the pyramids. Violet was also aware of the use of PI in many mathematical legends.

She recognized its relationship in many structures. The use of this math wonder hundreds, if not thousands of years before it's recognized discovery by Euclid is without question. Yet in today's world if things like this are mentioned it goes against the reigning paradigm and is not accepted by the scientific elite.

"What?" Eric asked himself, "Are they afraid to think outside the box."

Here again we have living proof that no one will look at. No wonder it is taking us so long to advance. This lost civilization before us was far more advanced a few thousand years ago then we are now.

Eric shook himself out of the wondering mode. *"Why do I do that to myself all the time,"* he thought.

Back to the air photo's. Perhaps he could learn more of this ancient village they would be visiting soon.

~~~~~~

Dove of Spring was truly wrapped up in her desire to be the Queen. She wanted everything as realistic as possible. Diego was also at his best in helping to create this image. He worked out the perfect headdress to look exactly like the elongated and flattened head of the Golden Lady. In his own mind he marveled at the similarity of this head shaping both for the Maya and Egyptian royalty though they
~~~~~~

were thousands of miles apart. His manufactured head dress was a perfect fit for Violet. So perfect you could not tell the difference between her and the photo of the Golden Lady. She only wished Whispering Wind could see this.

While the costume preparation was going on Mario was coaching Violet in some basic Maya tongue. Just a few simple things she could use with the children and the women.

Violet, because of her desire to be real, was a very fast learner. She already knew more than Eric who had been with his friends for many years.

In just short of a week she felt confident enough for her visit. Mateo along with Lone Buffalo set off early one morning to prepare the ancients for the Queen's visit. A day and time was finally set. In two days Violet's excitement would finally come to fruition. All were happy for her.

Carlos was working closely with Eric studying the layout of the small village. Small, anyhow compared to the very large spread of the complex they all had been examining for years.

Eric was extremely interested in the new structure he found with the aerial shots. It was no specific thing, just a gut feel because of its layout and position off set from the main pyramid of this tiny village. Both he and Carlos agreed this would not be easy because of this ever important leader of this group. At least ever important to himself. They both felt he was hiding or protecting something. They did, however, consider his protectiveness as a carry over or throw back to the Spanish invasion and destruction.

As was normal for the group all pitched in for the final preparations for the upcoming day. It was also agreed that Eric, Carlos, Diego and Mario would accompany Violet into the village. Mateo and Dan would remain close by but outside the village confine. This was for emergency purposes. Not that they expected any but they wanted to be prepared for any contingency.

Chapter 13

The big day finally arrived noticeably with six Spanish lance equipped escorts waiting just outside the archway to the King's complex. This time all were not frightened knowing Colonel Ramirez was most likely nearby.

The six escorts bowed humbly before the Queen as she left the complex. Violet felt confident in the part she was playing. After all she thought, this was in her blood.

It was almost a three hour walk to this ancient compound which Violet took in stride. Her queenly demeanor was steadfast and we all acted accordingly.

This time Eric did not carry the kings scepter, nor did he dress as the king. He wore regular clothes of the period as did the others. He only hoped the head man did not recognize him. This was Violet's show so we knew all eyes would be on her.

As they drew closer to the village the lance escort fanned out and almost disappeared into the jungle. A few children were just outside the confines of the settlement and as soon as they spotted the queen they smiled and squealed as little children so often do and turned and ran in to the village proper. We all got a kick out of their antics.

As we entered the village proper we put on serious faces and let the Queen have her honors. As the young ones hid shyly behind their mothers the head man, scepter and all, bowed respectfully to the queen. Violet bowed her head in return and proceeded to walk right past him. He appeared slightly annoyed until Carlos engaged him quickly in conversation.

Diego followed Violet almost as a servant. His child like personality was a perfect fit with the children. After a brief meeting with the women Dove of Spring parted with the children following to a clearing just outside the living area.

Mario engaged the head man in some serious conversation while leading him away from Carlos and me. This left us somewhat free to wander to the structure I saw on the photography. It was about a fifteen minute walk but we appeared to be alone. Buried in the jungle grasses that were reclaiming that space was a rectangular type pyramid, but flat topped, similar to where we found the Golden Lady.

Without actually measuring the sides they appeared to have a mathematical relation. The long sides were exactly two times that of the shorter sides. We felt the alignment matched the main structure and also the Kings tomb. The angled sides were smooth which prohibited climbing. This was sort of a disappointment. We circled this well made building twice before finding what we considered an opening. In short order using his magic fingers Carlos revealed a sliding rock portal allowing entrance.

Without hesitation we entered and using our pocket flash lights illuminated a most unexpected sight. One vast open space interrupted only by one stone pyre centered along one of the long walls but at least ten feet away from the wall itself. This structure we guessed to be six foot by eight foot and stood three feet high. Except for this one, alter shall we say, this was just one large spacious room.

"**A** holy place," Carlos said almost in a whisper. "Let's check all around," he added.

Simultaneously we both stepped forward which triggered the ever present lighting system we had become so acquainted with. He started on the alter like display while I proceeded a detailed search of the entire room. Except for the entrance I could not find any seams or cracks to indicate portals or other type of openings.

Carlos, however, was more successful.

"Eric, come look at this," he called.

As I reached him he pointed to what looked like a very fine line in the smooth stone running vertically. We both then proceeded with a more detailed search of that area. Almost at the same time we both called out at having identified other seams. His running vertically while mine ran horizontally. We smiled together.

Again Carlos put his magic touch fingers to work. He patiently searched for almost ten minutes. We were both so quiet that you almost could not hear our breathing. At last the familiar sound of stone on stone. Our smiles now turned into huge grins. We were now looking at descending steps, well made and smooth.

Before descending we closed the entry door to keep out uninvited guests. Namely the head man.

We bent into the entrance portal and slowly descended into darkness. As was my habit I counted thirty steps when we touched bottom. Here again our magic lighting came on.

Here, as in the kings tomb , was rack after rack of shelving. These shelves held what had to be thousands of scrolls and other isles of shelves held actual books. There had to be hundreds of them.

Carlos even voiced, jokingly, that this had to be the South American library of Alexander the Great..

We were both frozen in place for the longest time absorbing what was before us.

Without saying a word we both headed in opposite directions. Carlos to the scrolls and I to the books. I almost did not want to believe what I was viewing. Actual bound, hard cover books. Not the binding we are accustomed with but obviously a long lasting permanent bond. I hesitated almost not wanting to touch them but I finally gave in. Arbitrarily I reached for one. I could have sworn I felt a tingle when I touched it. I know that was strictly my imagination yet the thought of touching a piece of history thrilled me. I wiped my hands on my shirt not wanting to dirty these gems of the past.

Carefully opening the cover I was staring at a writing that of course I had never seen before. It wasn't a script as we know it today but it was an almost cursive style intermixed with obvious Glyph's

Oh, how I wished I could read it. I gingerly turned a few pages to see all kinds of styles of writing. A few pages even held sketches or designs on them. About halfway through the book I did recognize some drawings. They were depictions of stars or star placements along with what I believed to be the moon. I was so excited my hands were shaking so that I almost dropped the book. I wanted to shout, laugh and cry all at the same time but allowed some maturity to take hold and calmed down.

Eric looked over to Carlos who was also smiling, not at Eric but at whatever he was reading. He turned his attention back to the books. He very carefully returned the book to its place and reached for another one. One that was just as startling. This was filled with drawings. Reproductions of pyramids, stelae, statues and animals. This was an art book that should be in a museum for all to see he thought.

The art itself appeared to be done with a pointed charcoal pencil of sorts. This almost was as professional as any today. Shadings and shadows showed depth and angular perspective. Turning the many pages each drawing was better than the previous.

Eric came to a picture of a jaguar that looked so real he expected it to jump off the page at him.

For the next half hour silence was only broken by the turning of a page or the unrolling of a scroll.

Carlos was the first to call an end to the reading.

"We had better return to the others. Our absence may cause suspicions."

Eric knew he was right, but hated to leave this treasure trove of information.

They exited this library securing the door and even taking the time to erase their presence near the building by brushing away their trail.

They returned to the village as innocently as possible. Luck was with them, no one had noticed their absence.

Not a word was shared between Carlos and Eric on the return to the village though each was bursting with excitement. They were both anxious to see how Dove of Spring was doing with the children.

As they returned to the village compound Mario still had the head man engaged in conversation. Mario was just the man to do that thought Eric. The pair managed to signal Mario of their return to a great expression of relief on his face. He soon joined them as they headed for the open area to check on Violet. The three smiled as they approached because of the excitement and laughter of the young ones. Apparently the Queen and her aide had total control over the young ones. They were laughing as much as the young ones. Diego managed a signal to Carlos of about another half hour.

The three moved away slowly eyes forever working the compound. Eric in particular looking at the alter area where he almost lost his head.

Eventually they returned to the main pyramid. The head man, now without the scepter, which was a good sign, was with a group of men who all appeared to be relaxed and smiling. Mario returned to the leader while Eric and Carlos sort of lost themselves to the rear of the group engaging in small talk. Eric managed to remain quiet yet vigilant of every detail of the village. His only thought was to return to the library. He knew it would take months of research to discover what was really contained there.

Even that was going to involve negotiations with the headman who was so protective of everything. Rightfully so though considering the Spanish and their disregard and destruction of what was not theirs. Eric then made the correct decision, for now, to wait until all these factors are discussed by all. Who knows, perhaps with luck something will work out to our advantage.

Back to reality he told himself. I will go check on Violet again. He and Carlos had the same idea and they both headed to the sound of the children. As they neared the laughter Violet happened to look up and made eye contact with Eric who smiled at the sparkle in her eyes. He was obviously very happy for her.

The women standing on the side away from the action were all smiles and also appeared extremely happy

It was only minutes after that when Dove of Spring

called an end to the games much to the disappointment of the children.. She did indicate they should continue, it was only her participation that was ending.

Violet then walked to the mothers. With Diego as interpreter she suggested the mothers also participate in the games as she did.

The Queen then politely took her leave. Each mother in turn took the queens hand and bowed. Violet acknowledged each bow with a nod of her head and turned to the village with Diego obediently following.

The gathered men and women almost on Que separated to clear a pathway for the Queen bowing as they moved aside. Violet walked directly to the head man. He did not execute a complete bow but he did bow his head. To the surprise of us all she hooked the arm of the self important man and walked to the large pyramid. Some mumbling could be heard but no exact words were identified. The pair entered the structure leaving us all speechless.

Within five minutes they reappeared. This time the Queen was holding a book of sorts. Mr. Importance smiled and bowed deeply to Violet who then turned and with a nod of her head followed Diego to the jungle path. Mario, Carlos and Eric quickly followed not really knowing why.

Almost five minutes into the jungle they were joined by Dan and Mateo. And yet another five minutes passed and we were flanked by our lance carrying escorts. All were silent.

The hush reigned for the trek back to the kings tomb. As the Queens entourage passed through the archway our lanced escort turned and disappeared into the green of the jungle.

We all turned to Violet who was by now one big smile. She plopped down into a chair at the dinning table and let out a huge sigh of relief.

"Thank you gentlemen for letting this lady have the biggest thrill of her lifetime. I can't say when I have had this much enjoyment. Those children were the most precious thing that ever happened to me. I really do feel like a queen."

She was surrounded by all who were genuinely

congratulating her. Dan brought out a hidden bottle of Cognac and poured her a glass.

"You deserve this my Queen."

"I really need this now." she smiled as she accepted the glass and took a rather large sip.

"You were magnificent my love." praised Eric. "We are all proud of you."

"Don't be so stingy with the Cognac Dan," said Mario "We shall all toast our Queen."

Soon all were toasting Dove of Spring.

"Is our escort gone yet ?" She was looking towards the archway.

Diego ran to double check. He returned in a few minutes.

"Not a trace of them."

"Good" laughed Violet as she gladly removed her queens headdress.

"It's good to be free again."

"Okay. Now my lady don't keep us in suspense any longer. How did you get the book?"

Violet laughed, "I'm sorry, I almost forgot. In my limited Mayan with some Egyptian words and Spanish words mixed in I simply asked if I could borrow it for a short time. I wanted to check on some planned history to make sure everything is going according to expectations so as not to displease the Gods. I don't believe he has even read it or if he did he could not understand it. From the way he acted with me I think he is only ruling these poor people by fear. I don't think we will have any problem with him."

She finished with her winning smile.

"That's my girl," Eric said proudly.

"Where were you four or five years ago?" stated Mario.

Diego added his own thoughts.

"To celebrate, I'm going fishing for tonight's dinner which I will even cook."

Dan volunteered to join him.

It wasn't long before Diego and Dan returned with a bountiful catch. They immediately turned to in the cleaning and preparation for dinner. In the meantime Violet changed into more comfortable clothes. Eric and Carlos agreed to wait till after dinner to review their discovery with the others.

Dinner over they all pitched in for the clean up. Returning to the table Carlos became serious. He outlined their visit to what they now referred to as the library.

"This my friends appears to me to be untouched. I believe it is our good fortune that the Spanish missed this small out of the way structure. I believe Eric will agree with me that we two were the first ones to enter this treasure trove in possibly hundreds of years."

Eric nodded in agreement.

"When I say treasure trove I do not mean gold, silver and the like. The Kings Tomb provided us with enough of that. This building is what we would call a library. I even jokingly said this had to be the South American version of the Library of Alexander the Great. Books and Scrolls beyond imagination. This may give us some answers to our lost heritage and the lost civilization."

Everyone was all ears now. You could see the questions in their eyes.

"I will let Eric speak to you in a few moments. To continue, I only looked at a few scrolls. But even these few startled me, I believe they were written by our ancestors of hundreds of years ago. This is going to take many months of study and decipherment. These precious words could be our future. I don't mean we few here, but I mean our planet if it is even accepted."

This last statement drew the expected snickers.

"I will leave it there for now. More to come later. I'm sure Eric is as anxious as I to tell of his findings."

Eric nodded to Carlos and took a deep breath.

"I am as excited as Carlos with what I found. While he took to the scrolls I was drawn to the books."

The word books drew raised eyebrows from the group.

"Yes, I said books. Hard cover bound books. Admittedly I could not read much of what they contained but I did manage to grasp a few points. With the proper translation we may have answers to even the unasked questions. Questions not only of our past but as Carlos hinted, our future. I do feel these bound books will give us the information we not only need but want. Information of our past we never knew existed.

Eric took a breath here and with a loving smile and looking directly at Violet added;

"And we can thank our Egyptian connection for this."

Glasses were again raised to the queen. Mario then took this opportunity to speak.

"Now that we have heard from our two sleuths, it is time for our precious lady to tell us of her day.

Not really shy any more with this group she accepted the acknowledgment.

"My day was absolutely perfect. In fact I learned a few things also. These youngsters, particularly the boys already had their own version of Hop Scotch. Something they have been doing for who knows how many years. They would draw boxes or circles on the ground, not exactly in a straight line, and then they took turns throwing their favorite rocks starting with the closest box and working their way out. It was like a competition but not really. I gathered it was an exercise to hone their hunting skills. The mothers basically confirmed this."

Here Carlos politely interrupted,

"This must have been a practice of the ancient ones. It was not carried ahead to my generation. Sorry, Violet for the interruption."

Violet smiled in answer.

"I also want to take this opportunity to thank Diego for all his help. Not just for the costume but for his direct help in the games. I don't know who had the most fun. These children or Diego."

"I never really did grow up," smiled Diego in answer.

All agreed with him.

Eric spoke up again.

"Before we go our own ways again I would like to talk about this newly discovered library again. What do we do with this fountain of past knowledge. I agree with Carlos. I don't believe any one recent has been there. When I say recent I mean hundreds of years. The major problem now is how do we get access to it. I don't even think the head man knows of its worth, and if he did he is not likely going to allow us unlimited access. We also are aware of there lance carrying guards always in the area which prohibits our trying to sneak in. This could be the find of the century but we won't know that until we study everything. So, that being the case, the big question is how do we go about this without causing trouble."

Here Eric stopped and looked at all the questioning faces.

Mateo broke the momentary silence.

"What ever happened to our research in finding old Mayan settlements. That was almost easy work. Now we are into Lost Civilizations, tunnels to who knows where, outer space worm holes here on inner earth and libraries of old. This is not a complaint, just an obvious observation. We are only a few, how do we accomplish all this research?"

He then added with a half laugh,

"Teaching back at our Arizona college was almost easy by comparison."

There were chuckles all around. Mario added to Mateo's statement.

"Well if you think back a few years this is all Eric's fault. If he had not started talking to the king none of this would be happening."

The group, including Violet all turned to stare at Eric.

"Oh! So it's pick on Eric day again. Just for that no more Cognac."

"That's not fair." protested Dan. "I had nothing to with this. I'm going back to the reservation."

Laughing along with the others Dove of Spring raised her hand to speak.

"Gentlemen I'll go back to my earlier statement. We

quietly conduct our research on one thing at a time. I'm sure they will all come together at some point."

"I hate logical people." mumbled Diego , of course with a laugh.

There was momentary silence. Carlos again took the lead.

"Violet is right again. We take one step at a time and obviously this is not going to be any overnight success. Now back to what Eric questioned. Are there any ideas of how we get back to the library?"

Mateo hesitated before speaking. You could tell he was still thinking of something.

"How about another tunnel? We already have them running every which way. Why not from the King's home here to that ancient village?

There was total silence for a moment finally broken by Mario.

"That almost makes sense. Consider all the hidden things we already know about right here in the King's tomb. Could it be we missed a few very secret panels? Eric, with your photos, why not plot some sort of line to the library. The rest of us will start a very detailed search here at the King's tomb. Who knows what we may or may not find."

Agreement slowly passed from face to face. Mario continued,

"Okay. It's settled then. We start first thing tomorrow after a good nights rest."

Dan ended the evening with,

"But first another round of Cognac."

No one refused.

Chapter 14

The alarm clock Howler monkeys had everyone up early to a leisurely breakfast. Diego was the last to join the group.

"Some day I'm going to have that monkey for my breakfast," he said grumpily.

"None of us would ever get any work done then. We would be sleeping the day away," answered Mario, of course with a smile.

Enjoying their thick brewed coffee they made their plans for the day. Carlos and Mario would go over the King's tomb again to hopefully locate a missed portal. Diego and Dan would follow a projected imaginary line from the main pyramid to the ancient village looking for any sign of pathways. Mateo would stay at the complex keeping watch and updating journals. That left Hunter of Stories and Dove of Spring to follow as straight a line as possible Eric had plotted from the air photos also looking for any sign what so ever of a former presence.

Breakfast over and cleanup finished each went about their own assignments.

Even though Dan and Diego were basically headed in the same direction as Eric and Violet they were fanned out quite a bit. Eric was on a more direct route following land marks he identified on the air photos Violet was about ten or so feet ahead of Eric, her vigilant eyes not missing one bit of jungle growth.

Something actually did catch her eye. She carefully parted some of the jungle greenery exposing a moss covered stelae.

She immediately called to Eric. While waiting she started to brush away some of the moss. She was instantly taken in by the Glyph carving. The beauty of the design she could not help but admire.

"And the Spanish considered them a backwards and ignorant people," she thought.

Eric was now at her side as fascinated as she. The pair spent the next ten minutes clearing away the jungle growth totally exposing the magnificence of this work of art. They both identified the Orion complex among the many engravings.

"And this I take to be Venus," said Eric.

He based his identification on what Dan had pointed out from his star charts.

While Eric conducted an in depth study of all sides of the stelae, Violet moved away still eye balling every thing possible. Nothing really escaped her view. She felt this jungle was becoming her teacher and wanted to know everything there was to know. Nothing escaped her eyes.

Having done a pretty thorough job of cleaning this carved beauty Eric stood back somewhat studying all there was to see. The quietude of his mind was suddenly interrupted.

"Your coming was foretold to me ages ago."

Although he was familiar with thought transfer he was taken aback by this voice in his head. He was not familiar with the obvious accent. He stood there frozen in place. A short time passed and the voice spoke again.

"Do not be alarmed. You are the Chosen One to receive my message. Is it not true that you are a disciple of Atl. That you carry on his mission."

Without realizing it Eric was answering.

"Yes. He and I reviewed many things and yes he directed me to fulfill his mission. Yet I never really knew what the full extent of that was which is why I am still searching.

"Search no more Oh Chosen One. Your answers are here with me. I have been waiting for you for untold time. What I have to pass on is much yet will take little of your time. We will continue when we are alone."

As with Atl the voice faded away. It was then Eric realized Violet was standing next to him.

"Are you okay Eric? You appeared to be up in a cloud somewhere."

He looked at Violet but remained silent.

She pushed no further.

Eric remained starring at nothing in silence. Violet was slightly upset but chose not to force the issue. She knew Eric well enough that he would come around sooner or later. She was thankful she had patience for the man she loved.

A distant screech of some unknown bird shook him out of his mental stupor.

"I'm sorry my love but I just had a surprising experience. A voice from the past just spoke to me."

"I thought you said Atl went to his forever sleep.'

"Yes, that is true, but this was not Atl. It was he who Atl was searching for and chose me to continue the search. Well I guess the search is finally over."

What did this voice relay to you?"

"Nothing really. He detected your presence and chose not to speak. He obviously did not know your connection to me or to this whole dream we are involved with."

"Then I will move away so that you may continue."

"No stay with me for now. I will return here later alone. Right now I need you with me."

He reached for her hand and held it tightly. To change the subject Eric asked,

"Well did you discover any other wonders my Queen?"

Smiling now knowing the subject has been dropped

she answered cheerfully,

"Not a thing. One stelae a day is enough for me."

They both laughed as they hugged.

"Let's continue on our journey, who knows what else we may find," Eric suggested as he tugged her by the hand.

The rest of the day proved to be nothing. On the return to the complex Eric stopped to take some GPS readings to plot on his photo's and master map. They were the first to return and went straight to the coffee pot. Within twenty minutes the others drifted in. Eric was sitting alone his mind drifting to all that had taken place over the last few years. Dove of Spring was the only good thing that happened to him, not that he didn't appreciate what he had learned. The jungle is wonderful but his life was being taken in too many directions at this point.

"Why has all this been thrust on me?" He puzzled. *"I am just another John Doe like anybody else, not a Chosen One. Chosen by who? People I can't see."*

Here Eric scolded himself yet again.

"Relax Eric, you chose to be here, you weren't put here." He looked around and smiled. "I do like being here."

He waited till all were gathered around the table before he spoke. With coffee all around and all seated comfortably Violet started the debriefing of the day.

"I came across another stelae today that was quite well hidden. Eric and I spent quite a lot of time undoing the jungles reclamation efforts. I will let Eric fill you in on the rest."

Eric sat there, his mind still drifting elsewhere until Violet touched his shoulder.

"Huh, oh yeah, the stelae. Just like the others we have come across I could not read the Glyph's or inscriptions. But..."

Here he hesitated looking at all eyes starring at him. Slowly he described the size and design of the four sides.

He hesitated yet again then finally spoke normally.

"Just like the King, a voice entered my mind. It

appeared to know me or at least of me and was expecting me. He said he had much to share with me." He paused here again trying to sort things out in his mind.

"Well don't stop now. What did he say?" quizzed Mario excitedly.

"He wouldn't say anything more. He detected Violet's presence and faded away just as the King always did saying we would talk later when I was alone. Then he was gone. Violet and I continued our searching for a while then returned here. I will return there alone tomorrow."

The group was excited but obviously disappointed.

"Hurry up and wait. That's all we ever do with you," joked Diego.

Carlos then spoke of his searches with Mario.

"We pretty well fine tooth combed most of the pyramid inside to no avail. We still have the treasure room to do and then perhaps the outside perimeter. As I stated before we found nothing."

Diego and Dan reported pretty much the same.

Mateo then spoke of his exciting day trying to stay awake.

"If it was not for the Howler monkeys I would probably still be sleeping."

"Once again it seems we have our Queen to thank for another promising discovery," smiled Carlos.

Violet appeared slightly embarrassed but deep inside was proud of herself that she could contribute to their efforts. She herself was now deeply involved in this Lost Civilization and Lost World drama.

The rest of the late afternoon was planning for the next day, an early supper and it was time for the jungle serenade. Eric and Violet did find some alone time to just relax and listen to the music of the jungle.

"At least there are more than three trees in the jungle," Violet quipped.

The next day was a cool ninety one degrees which everyone was pleased with. Eric headed out early to the new found stelae wondering what message there may be.

Carlos and Mario continued to comb the kings tomb interior. Dan and Mateo took on the outside search of the pyramid following the instructions of Carlos of what to look for.

This left Diego and Violet for camp duty this day. Violet really wanted to be with Eric but understood the importance of him being alone.

She and Diego cleaned house so to speak. Fresh coffee and dinner prep were almost routine now after these past four years.

Diego quietly signaled to Dove of Spring to make herself scarce. He heard some noise from the jungle outside the compound and had not identified it yet. Violet complied and hid herself as best she could. Diego slowly inched his way to the archway with a hidden revolver in his pocket. As he neared the entrance he heard a familiar voice.

"Ah, Senor` Diego, I am glad to see you are alert."

Diego relaxed as he recognized Colonel Ramirez. Violet also recognized the voice and started for the archway.

"Buenos Dias my Queen. I am glad to see you as well. We are on our usual daily patrols but I wanted to see you personally. Actually all of you but you in particular."

Violet was puzzled by his words until Ramirez continued.

"I personally wanted to thank you for your visit to the ancient ones. The children are still reliving your time with them. You gave them something special because of your attention to them. This is something they will never forget. The whole village is still reliving the experience. My never ending gratitude my Queen. You have been a blessing to my people."

He said these words along with a genuine bow of respect.

"I will bother you no more, I have patrolling yet to be accomplished. I will take my leave now. Via con Dios to you both."

With that he melted into the jungle.

Violet could feel herself blush as she watched the colonel fade away. Looking to Diego she said

"Much of that praise also belongs to you my friend. I could not have done it without you. My sincere thanks."

Now even Diego was blushing. Quickly to change the subject he voiced

"We had better start working on supper or we will both be in real trouble."

Both laughing now they started for the kitchen area

Chapter 15

Eric approached the stelae not knowing what to expect. He circled it three or four times admiring the art work. Art work of so long ago the Spanish could not believe it was from these primitive people. He drew closer for a better look at a Glyph that he thought unusual. The voice from within spoke.

"I feel you are alone. That is good. What I have to say is for your ears only. Near here lies a repository of knowledge. A wisdom unknown to these of this present world. We Chosen Ones have been keepers of this intelligence for eons."

Here Eric interrupted.

"I don't mean to be rude. I am anxious to know of this knowledge but I know not of its origin. That information will be most helpful in the further dissemination of these truths."

"Atl did not tell you where he came from?"

"No, Atl and I shared many things yet never the original source."

"Eons ago, when Earth was still young and forming, these live beings of a super intelligence far beyond what you can only hope to attain, we had what you today would call a continent. It was not far from

where we presently stand. Just east of here are many islands in the waters that you call the Carribean. These islands were at earlier times mountain peaks of our homeland. A homeland advanced in the arts, sciences, astronomy and architecture and what you now call mathematics. We were known as the continent of Atlantis. A name I'm sure you are familiar with."

Eric chimed in again.

"I don't mean to be rude but the present belief of today's world totally doubts the existence of Atlantis. It is said to be just old folklore of the past."

There was a pause. My invisible Chosen One finally continued.

"Here again is knowledge your people of your time refuse to accept. This has been a problem to all of us that were Chosen Ones to freely disseminate our wisdom. Atlantis did exist. The end of the last Ice Age, some twelve thousand years ago caused floods beyond imagination. Half of the worlds land mass was swallowed by the rising seas. It was total destruction and annihilation for many lands and peoples. It was so sudden few escaped. We knew this was coming which we than chose a few to carry our knowledge to other of lands undisturbed by the waters. Your King, that you call Atl, was one of these emissaries. His teachings, as with the rest of us were falling on deaf ears. Hence your backwardness by comparison. Now does that answer your inquisitiveness?"

Eric could almost detect annoyance in this mystery voice yet he could understand why. Doubt from so many for so long would lead to that mind set.

"I apologize for my ignorance but as with Atl I am here to learn."

Eric could feel a mood change and knew he said the right thing. He was here to learn.

The voice continued,

"Now back to where I started, and without interruption. Near here lyes a repository of knowledge. It is one of the few the Spanish never found. Here are books and scrolls of all things necessary for advancement this planet so badly needs. Advancement not based on war and destruction but on scientific theorems of the universe. We are just one mere spec in a never ending and ever expanding universe. Our people studied the sun, moon and stars. Venus, as you have surmised was very important to us, as it was to some before us and a few after us. The mathematics of the astronomy is ever important to the future of this globe. Your future. If used wisely and without greed your future will be one of true peace and advancement. But if in the hands of a few power hungry beings the world as you know it will most likely see absolute destruction and life will no longer exist. Not just human life but all life. Are there any questions so far?"

Eric was so taken aback that he could not speak properly.

"N, N, No. I guess not at this time."

There was total silence, even the jungle sounds ceased. Quietly the voice in his head continued and less antagonistic.

"Study this ancient wisdom and amazing things will be revealed."

Eric started to speak but thought better of it not wanting to interrupt again. This now new teacher must have read his thoughts.

"Yes, our way of construction of these

pyramids and temples will also be revealed. It was used throughout this planet."

There was a pause, then the voice, in a softer tone relayed its feelings.

"I am growing weary now. I must rest. We will speak again another time."

The voice faded into the forest.

Eric stood there eyes fixated on a Glyph. He remained motionless. How long he did not know. Slowly the ever sweet sounds of the jungle returned and with time Eric returned to the present. He remained a while longer but the voice did not return. He, without rushing made his way back to the others. His mind a blur of confusion. As he walked through the archway he could smell the coffee and knew that was what he needed and wanted.

Violet was the first to notice he was back. She rushed to him like a school girl. First a hug and a kiss then she sat next to him.

"How did everything go? No wait, don't say anything yet, let me get some coffee." She returned with her mug of black syrup and enthusiastically repeated., "How did everything go?"

Eric hesitated before speaking and was then interrupted by the others returning. They all headed straight to Eric.

"Okay," said Mario. "Don't keep us in the dark."

Eric half smiled at this yet still hesitated.

"I don't really know how to begin."

"Did you get to speak to the Chosen One?"

"Yes," was all Eric replied.

"Well what did you learn?"

"Not very much. The voice just rambled on as we so often do. He spoke of many things but really said nothing."

"Now even you are starting to sound like the King talking in riddles," Diego interjected.

"I'm sorry," smiled Eric. "It's just that it was a very

confusing morning. The only positive thing in our conversation was a confirmation of the library we found. According to my voice it holds the wisdom of the ages. Perhaps not all because the Spanish did destroy so much. There apparently is another registry of these books and scrolls still well hidden. Its location was not disclosed to me, Yet. We should be able to learn more of their math and astronomy. These two subjects appear to be the key to their advancement. Yes, there are other ingredients but this is the main thrust of their wisdom. According to the voice the knowledge goes back eons of time. To before the last ice age."

Here Eric paused again reaching for his coffee. He quickly gazed at Violet who smiled and gave him a wink of love and confidence. He almost did not believe how good this made him feel. He quickly recalled the words of Whispering Wind. *"She will always be there for you."*

Mateo finally spoke up.

"**Y**ou mean you spent all that time for just that little information?"

Half laughing now Eric answered,

"**I** told you at the outset of this it was a hectic time. He spoke non-stop for a while complaining, as we do, that their message was falling on deaf ears. He loosely referred to Venus and its importance to them yet at the same time he was really saying nothing. He did speak with negativity about things, if not changed, will be the end of us all. Then to top it all he cut our dialogue short because he was growing weary and tired. He needed rest. He did however indicate that we would talk again. When that will be I have no clue. I will just keep trying. I did , however, get the indication that he will not be with us much longer. The signs are there just as with the King. I will try again tomorrow. Wish me luck. I hope the rest of you had better success."

Carlos accepted this as his turn to speak.

"**W**e, unfortunately had no better luck. We left no crack or hole or scratch uninspected in detail. We double checked each other constantly. I don't believe there is another hidden passage in that tomb pyramid."

Diego jumped in here.

"We found absolutely nothing also. We also retraced pathways leaving no leaf unturned. There are no other trails or any signs that there ever were."

"Well, at least we still have the library," Eric ended with. "Now gentlemen, if you don't mind, I need some rest. I have had enough brain drain for today."

With that he smiled, waved goodbye and headed for his sleep area followed by a concerned Dove of Spring.

As soon as Eric reached his destination he settled into his hammock. A serious Violet softly said,

"We can always go home you know."

What! And leave the find of the millennium to millennium doubters of the world. Not on your life."

He finished with a smile.

Wake me for dinner."

Violet kissed him gently and returned to the others.

"Is he alright?" Mario asked right away.

"I'm sure he will be. He has had bouts with this before. This Chosen One stuff weighs heavily on his mind. Sometimes I think he takes it too seriously. I know he wants to see it through. He dearly loves you guys and wants to help in every way he can. But I believe he allows it to take control of him. That's just my opinion. Please don't tell him I said anything. He is a very proud man."

Now smiling slightly she added.

"And in case you hadn't noticed you have me won over one hundred percent. I will do all in my meager power to assist you to attain your goal."

Carlos, also now smiling answered.

"We have not noticed any impact from you. We thought you were here just for a vacation. On the serious side now, you are definitely one of us and we are extremely thankful for that. We will see what we can do to take some of the pressure from him. He has done more than his share already. We would not be this far had it not been for him."

A rush of pride ran through Violet.

While Eric was getting his much deserved rest the remaining six made rough plans for the next day. Violet chose to stay home again but she would continue some air photo research. Having said this she received quizzical looks from the others. Smiling she answered the unasked question.

"Yes, before we came here Eric gave me a few quick lessons in how and what to look for. Being a practiced engineer I was not unfamiliar with his field. Even he was surprised at how quickly I caught on."

Mario, in a cheerful tone said,

"Frank would have loved to hear you say that. He was always at a total loss with that."

Diego said his stomach was reminding him to eat again. They all pitched in and Bingo dinner was ready. Violet went to get Eric who was just arousing. To dinner they went.

During dinner Eric firmly stated,

"I am going back tomorrow and this time I will get answers."

The group looked rather shocked at his statement. Smiling he explained further.

"Not to worry, I will not spoil it for us. I think it will just be a matter of talking a different way. Yesterday I let him run the show, today I will. In a nice way, of course," he added.

They all knew Eric's determination on certain matters so the subject was dropped for the evening.

Dan volunteered to go fishing again. No one disagreed as long as he promised to do the cleaning and cooking. Before he could protest they all got up from the table and turned to on cleanup.

It was now rest time. Time for Eric's music of the night.

Early rise the next morning for Violet and Eric. While Violet fixed the coffee Eric set up a few strips of photography for her to see what she could locate.

Eric had a light meal but did take along a few power

bars for his day at the Stelae.

Chapter 16

Eric was determined to get answers from this Chosen One. He was not going to be antagonistic but he would remain firm and professional as possible.

His journey to the stelae was uneventful. There did not even appear to be the usual soft jungle noises. He thought that was quite odd. It was a totally quiet day. So far.

Finally arriving, he again took note of the unusual quiet. Waiting only a few minutes the voice of the past recognized his presence.

"I knew you would be back this soon. Atl had mentioned you were ever curious."

"Curious, yes!" Eric answered and today I would like to get answers, not just a history lesson."

"Atl also mentioned you could be stubborn."

Eric again answered right away.

"I do not mean it in a belligerent way. I am not by nature a n aggressive person, but I would like answers to my thoughts. I know by the signs and your personal own admission that you will be soon going to your forever sleep. I would like to learn whatever I can before that occurs. I hope we can co-operate with each other."

"I understand your concern. I reflected on those very concerns during your absence. As you said you are here to learn and so I am here to show what I can."

Eric felt better now. Taking a firm stand paid off. He relaxed somewhat and even softened his tone.

"To start with, in our research we have come across many tunnels leading to different structures. Can you shed any light on the how and why of them?"

"That is something I do not have much information on. I am not Maya but I am of their ancestry. The ancient ones from Atlantis are responsible for them. To what end or for what use was never divulged to us. What little we did uncover was that it had to do with the universe itself. Possible time travel. Our astronomical studies were well advanced but not yet to that level. As you are already aware our calendar is based on Venus along with the sun. It was and still is more accurate than that used by you today. That came about from thousands of years of planet and sun observations. Polar reversal and magnetic attraction between planetary bodies is all outlined in the books and scrolls that you discovered. How much is there I cannot say. The Spanish destroyed so much of our heritage. Once you have decoded our studies you will have more understanding of our advances. This may sound vague to you but that is all I can offer at this time. How much was recorded and of what I can not answer. Only your future study will tell."

Eric was not completely happy with this answer yet also believed the voice did not truly know.

Without further encouragement the voice continued.

"You may also find information on Solar radiation and sun spots. Some of this had relayed to us by those of Atlantis. I was not part of that but it was passed on to us and recorded in our books. Again whether or not any of this survived I do not know."

Frustrated by the lack of information but believing the voice Eric still pushed on.

There appears to be forever lighting in these underground tunnels. What can you share about that?"

"That was a great surprise to us also. I believe it is actually based on the collection of Solar energy and stored for future use as needed. Your people will have to study this system. I have no further knowledge of it. Again I repeat untold knowledge awaits you once you decipher our recordings."

"Is there anything else you can share to help us decipher these books?"

"Only that the Atlantians also were sharing with the Egyptians similar teachings. Which is why we have that Egyptian connection today. Our Mayan brethren learned more and faster then others based on their already advanced mathematics and astronomy. I wish you luck in your future to learn of these advances and continue to use this information. Remember though the whole concept is based on sharing equally with all and to eliminate the greed of the few. I wish I could say more but I feel my time is near. Do not give up your quest."

All was silent. Eric knew his contact faded into oblivion

Eric sat on the ground, his back resting against the

Stelae. He smiled to himself as he heard the all familiar sounds of the jungle return He felt disappointed yet satisfied at the same time. There future would still have to be taken a day at a time.

Eric sat there upwards of a half hour not even thinking of what just happened. His mind was elsewhere and everywhere. He recalled his first meeting with Dove of Spring. He drifted to his studio in Vermont. How simple his life was then.

"I could go back there," he thought.

He laughed when he also thought of losing his three tree jungle on the reservation. He did like it here in the Yucatan. Especially with Violet at his side. He even remembered his first sight of the King's tomb. How strange it all appeared.

The inevitable Howler monkey broke the jungle reverie. Eric munched on a power bar and viewed the stelae once more then headed for home. He took it slow returning, just enjoying his new world of peace.

As he entered the archway he was spotted by Dove of Spring who immediately ran to him almost knocking him over as she threw her arms around him.

"I was beginning to get concerned."

"No need for that. I'm a big boy now and can take care of myself."

Violet instantly put on a pout face saying, " Oh, so you don't need me any more."

Hugging her again, he laughingly answered.

"That's not what I said and you know it."

Dan's voice was heard from a distance.

"Knock it off you two, we have work to do."

The couple walked to a smiling Dan.

"Mario and Carlos are still searching the treasure room. Diego and Mateo are out searching for something Violet thought she picked out on the aerial shots."

Smiling Eric looked at Violet saying, "That's my girl."

"I'm most likely wrong, but I thought I saw something

that did not fit with the rest of the terrain. Diego and Mateo I think were getting bored so they decided to have a look. What about your day? Did you learn anything new?"

"Yes and no. Let' wait till everyone is here," Eric suggested. "In the meantime show me what you saw."

He took her hand and headed for the table where the photo's were.

"The glasses are still set on that location," she offered.

Eric sat down and lowered his head to the stereo viewer. Violet anxiously waited as he slid the glasses in all directions. He silently viewed for a few minutes and finally raised his head. He was wearing a smile.

"You have done it again my Queen. I can't say for certain but it looks as if this bit of jungle was cleared at one time. The cleared area that now exists has low growth. In other words no large trees. There may be a flat topped structure there or was there. Not a bad find for a beginner."

Deep inside Eric was actually proud of her. Getting the hang of aerial interpretation is not an easy thing. They would just have to wait for the return of the bored pair.

The three wandered over to the ever ready coffee pot Eric filled his mug and made himself comfortable. Dan went back to his star charts at the far end of the table leaving Eric and Violet some privacy which was soon suspended with the return of Diego and Mateo.

Of course the first thing asked was did Eric learn anything new. Again he put it off until all were present. Instead Eric asked his questions which surprised them both.

"This clearing, if you found it, did it have an open flat area or perhaps show signs of a structure?"

"Yes, it did. How did you know?" questioned Diego.

"That's what I saw on the photos. I was just confirming what Violet thought she detected."

"You mean she was correct in her interpretation?" Mateo added.

"She was absolutely correct," Eric answered.

Then why do we need you?" asked Mateo.

Violet broke in to Eric's defense.

"Gentlemen, we can't get rid of Eric. Who would make the coffee then?"

All but Eric were laughing now.

"Oh great, I see it's Eric's turn in the barrel again. Just for that there will be no more Cognac. I'll just have to drink it all myself."

"What's this about Cognac?" Eric heard a voice behind him say.

Carlos and Mario just returned from the treasure room.

"Okay, debriefing time folks." announced Carlos as he headed for the table.

Coffee mugs filled and all were seated.

"I'll kick it off with our disappointing day. Mario and I spent our day going over that area with a super fine toothed comb. There is not a scratch that we did not super investigate. In fact, I think we probably left some additional scratches that were not there before. Believe me, my finger nails show it also. Even now I can see Eric ready to jump up and teach to us all he has been taught about our future."

Of course he said this sarcastically with a half grin. He could tell by the expression on his face that Eric was disappointed with his day. Eric now smiling himself responded immediately.

"You make it sound like I have the answers to the problems of the universe. Well not quite, unfortunately I don't. Truth be told I learned very little."

Disheartened expressions now showed all around. In fact that very instant a pair of Howler monkeys howled their laughs which lasted about five seconds.

Eric gazed upwards saying "Thank you my friends. I needed that."

Turning back to his friends he went on with his narrative.

"The voice knew almost nothing. Rather than being

an outreach Chosen One I got the feeling he was only a guardian of records. The bright side, if you want to call it that, is that when we decode all that is in this newly found library, we should have a plethora of answers to whatever questions we may now have."

Here he paused for a sip of his black syrup.

"On the bright side there is also another of these librarys that was untouched by the invading Spanish, but its location was unknown to him. The only other good thing of our talk was, and I know you are not going to want to believe it, the existence of the ever elusive Atlantis. According to my voice all this advanced knowledge came directly from the Atlantians. When their lands were taken by the rising seas their disciples went both east and west, hence the Egyptian connection. And now on a sad note to finish my presentation he, like the King, went to his forever rest."

"Well at least we now know what work we have waiting for us." Mario said seriously.

"How are we few going to accomplish the work of centuries let alone convince others?" asked Mateo.

There was silence which lasted a minute or so. Dan enthusiastically spoke out.

"Let's start recruiting others. You yourself have told of the many students at your university that are already helping with translations. Not to push myself on you but I can guess that my teens would love to be a part of this."

"Funding for all of this would present quite a problem," said the ever practical Mario.

Dan would not accept that as a reason not to try.

"Most of us are doing this at very little expense. I think that idea could be a shared thing. The results could mean a great deal to us and our world. I for one am not in this work for monetary gain. I enjoy what we are doing. To me that is payment enough. I only hope I can continue with you all. With my teens it will even be better."

Dan looked around at all the now smiling faces. Violet stood quietly.

"I think Dan is correct in what he said. I know the teens he is talking about and he is correct in his assessment. They would just love to tackle something like this. They are a group of very intelligent young people."

She ended with a wide grin.

"They will do most anything for Pizza."

This, of course brought big smile all around.

"**O**ur Queen has helped us again," said Carlos.

"That's not all she helped us with today," Diego interjected. She made another discovery today by doing Eric's job. Her success in the aerial photo interpretation brought us to another possible area of interest. Dan and I made a quick check on it today. I do believe it has possibilities.

For a non productive day it appears it was productive anyway. First dinner and then Cognac to celebrate," was put forth by Mario.

The evening was relatively short with quiet conversation of many different topics not work related. The music of the night slowly crept through the area and all succumbed to its call. Soon the only sound was the music.

~ ~ ~ ~ ~ ~

The next morning it was decided all would go to this new discovery by Violet. Included were machetes, shovels, camera, GPS and what ever other little thing they could each think of. It would either be a work busy day or one of relaxing enjoyment. There was just plain old no rush.

As they neared the site excitement overcame the seven. Each in their own way was assessing the possibilities of this new find. Encircling the area many times some ideas were discarded yet were replaced by others.

Carlos and Eric determined the top, under a thin layer of dirt and grass, was many purposefully placed stone. Digging and clearing commenced which included Dove of Spring. She willingly assumed her fair share. Eric, when not using his shovel was documenting all photographically.

After laboring for an hour or so they were seeing a flat topped structure. The top was guesstimated to be six feet by nine feet composed of large flat stone fitted together almost seamlessly. They all agreed this was most likely would be pyramid shaped. Shortly after, some test digging confirmed this yet did not dampen their enthusiasm. Digging recommenced, of course at a slower pace because of the downward angle.

Mario, on his break from digging decided Colonel Ramirez should be notified to make sure safeguards were in place for its protection from looters. Mateo volunteered to search him out.

The digging was slower now but they were making progress. Carlos suddenly called a halt to their effort.

"We may not have to go any deeper," he stated quietly.

Confusion registered on everyone's face. Carlos continued ignoring the looks.

"**W**hat I'm seeing right now could be an access door."

Eric instantly moved to Carlos who was already pointing to his place of interest.

"**L**ook over here," he said as he moved closer.

"**T**here appears to be a slight indent in the wall at that point," Eric said aloud.

"**E**xactly," Carlos confirmed.

Now both men were on their knees, hands and fingers working their magic. They hoped.

A long ten minutes passed when finally Cxarlos spoke louder than normal.

"Eric, look here!" as he fingers were already busy brushing dirt away.

Eric joined excitedly as the others looked on and moved closer. He suddenly moved his hands faster exposing the ever familiar Orion Complex. This design was becoming an old friend by now.

Violet was beaming a wide smile at this point. She felt a special relationship with this star configuration.

In the meantime, the ever clever Diego was collecting bunches of small twigs. Stiff twigs yet supple enough to be used as a broom. He moved to the place of interest and began sweeping. Much to the surprise of the others his work showed instant results. Other designs were revealing themselves. Again, like all other structures uncovered, this could be important and revealing of the past.

Eric backed off somewhat giving the master room to perform his finger magic. At the same time Mario and Dan were discussing ways to make this site disappear again. Diego did wonders on the "Golden Lady" site and they agreed it could be done a second time. Then again it all depended on what this structure showed once they gained access.

While Carlos was still trying with his finger technique, Violet softly and casually mentioned that just about everything in Egypt was opened with the Orion Belt Stars.

"Are those stars indented at all?"

At this stage of the game everyone trusted and listened to anything Violet suggested. Carlos carefully cleaned all the dirt from that area.

"Yes, they are recessed somewhat," he answered.

"Then push all three at the same time with equal pressure."

"And we will all keep our fingers crossed," added Mario.

Carlos did as instructed and sure enough the sound of stone on stone, which was familiar to all, could be heard. Except this time Carlos was not prepared to have the place he was standing move. It moved slowly but fast enough to knock him head over heel down the slope into a pile of dirt.

Dan was the first to reach him. Carlos appeared to be alright. Just embarrassed by his own stupidity knowing he was standing in the wrong place when he pushed on the three stars.

Once all calmed down they were looking at the opening of about three feet by five feet with the usual descending steps into darkness. They let the stale air dissipate before trying to go down. Mario volunteered to go first and had his pocket flashlight at the ready. When they agreed the air was stabilized enough Mario started his descent. Like all of the other structures this was no different. The steps were pretty regular in width and as was expected halfway down the lighting system engaged.

"Carlos jokingly said, "I didn't hear any screams yet so I guess everything is okay," he continued with, "Well Violet, since this is your discovery you may go next, the rest of us will follow."

She was thrilled with this recognition as she headed down and as was Eric's habit she counted the steps to the bottom. Both she and Mario looked around. There was nothing to see. A large room about eight foot square with a ceiling also about eight foot high.

"Which means," spoke Mario, "That one of these walls must have a corridor leading some where from it."

By now Eric, Carlos and Diego had joined them. Dan stayed topside to keep watch. The five below were all now scanning the walls for indications of portals. Diego spoke out.

"I have not seen any seams yet but there is a faint Glyph here that I have never seen before. I cannot read it."

They all took turns to see this Glyph. Violet with out hesitation announced,

"This is not a Maya Glyph as you know it. This is an Egyptian Cartouche. "

Carlos was stunned to hear this.

"Are you sure?" He questioned.

"Yes, I saw this very same thing on one of the small pyramid burial tombs when we were there. This was where Nefertiti was buried. This is another Egyptian connection to the Maya of old."

They all stared in disbelief.

"The world could not turn a deaf ear on them now. This is proof positive." she added.

"We are still going to have doubters." mumbled Carlos.

Everyone agreed but Violet.

"How can anyone doubt this?" she voiced aloud. "We will just have to convince them," she added innocently with a smile.

"You're positive attitude will help us all." answered Mario. "Now on with the search.

The group separated to different walls. Eric and Dove of Spring stayed with the cartouche. You could see Eric was deep in thought by his furrowed brow and squinty eyes. He walked to the steps then turned to face the Egyptian cartouche wall. Talking out loud to no one in particular, though they all heard, that wall is also in line to the home of the ancient ones and the library.

Carlos immediately started scanning for seams or markings. Eric joined him. All was quiet while they scanned the wall.

"Is this what you are looking for?" quizzed Violet as she pushed three fingers against the wall which slowly pivoted on a center point.

Stale air filled the room as each of them covered their faces with anything they could grab. One by one they headed for the steps.

A half hour or so of breathing fresh air they decided to reenter the underground. Only two went this time. The others would follow later. Eric and Carlos descended the steps hoping there guess was correct.

The others truly appreciated the rest and fresh air. Diego and Dan were again talking of making this site disappear. They determined it would be easier than the "Golden Lady's" door. They figured they would not have to do too much digging to start with.

Violet and Mario spoke more of her time in Egypt and the Nefertiti visit.

Chapter 17

Mateo returned accompanied by Colonel Ramirez and half dozen of his military men. Most were already familiar with the Archeological group and welcomed their efforts to discover and protect their history. They were all in awe of Violet as their queen even though they knew she was not the real queen. They knew the story of her ancestry and respected her because of it.

In the meantime while the group was resting, Carlos and Eric had almost completed their two hour journey and yes they did end up at the library, as they called it, in the ancient village. This delighted them no end. They now knew they could come and go all they wanted without the all important head man being any the wiser. They could now have some privacy in their research.

They carefully entered the library and each automatically returned to their previous locations. Carlos to the scrolls and Eric to the books. They did caution each other about the time of day and agreed not to dally too long. Their thoughts also harmonized to the point that each would take along one scroll and one book to show the others. This would give them time to study in more detail the contents. Who knows, possibly even decode some of it.

After twenty minutes of research each had a chosen text and started their return journey pleased that they did not have to deal with the village leader.

They were both relatively silent on the walk home just thinking about the contents they carried in their hands. They also were aware of the sharing necessary with the others. They could all possibly bring something to the understanding of these documents.

They automatically quickened their pace to get to the others as soon as possible.

Their return was happily welcomed and that included Colonel Ramirez. He and his men would stay the evening at the Kings Tomb complex. He too had an extreme interest in this library. He had heard of its existence many years ago but because of his dedication to the protection of such places, did not have time to pursue the history of his people. He was more than pleased with what this group was doing and would always be there for their protection.

His men were also happy to be part of this research and in turn promised to share whatever they could. They would even be more pleased to be interviewed as to their knowledge of their own history.

A small celebratory dinner and all relaxed speaking of what they hoped these books and scrolls would provide.

"I myself have much knowledge of our historical Glyphs which I am willing to share to rebuild the past of my people," stated the Colonel proudly.

Carlos and Mario on hearing these words were enthusiastically pleased and indicated to the Colonel they would take him up on his offer.

Based on that Diego also suggested they seek out others of their kinfolk who also may have a lost or hidden knowledge of their past.

The evenings conversation was positive all around. Even the music of the night was more soothing and positive as if the jungle was happy with the results of the night. It was decided that rest was in order knowing tomorrow was going to be a busy day. Perhaps not physically but busy just the same. The newly acquired book and scroll were locked away in the kings tomb for the night for safe keeping.

Eric was finally relaxed to the point that he looked forward to a good nights sleep. Even Violet was pleased for him. She smiled as she watched him close his eyes almost immediately and was gone for the night.

~ ~ ~ ~ ~ ~

Colonel Ramirez and his men left at sunrise to continue the safeguard patrol. Most of the others slowly emerged from the night of rest. Even the Howler monkey did not disturb them this morning. Naturally.

One by one they laggardly drifted into the world of reality. It was a good hour before they were all gathered around the table with the forever coffee mug. Breakfast was sort of take care of yourself if you wanted.

With all gathered and coffee alert the day was planned. Carlos and Mario would study the book since they were the two most knowledgeable of the Glyph symbols. Eric was naturally disappointed in this choice but did realize it was the logical decision. Mateo and Diego would study the scroll with periodic assistance from Eric. This left Lone Buffalo and Dove of Spring free to assist any one in any other way.

Violet temporarily satisfied herself with more Aerial photo studies. Dan went back for more detailed alignments of his star charts making the mathematical adjustments necessary taking into account hundreds of years from the past. For the whole morning the camp itself was quiet save for the normal day sounds of the surrounding jungle.

Violet was totally surprised with her viewing of the fascinating jungle surrounds in the third dimension. Now she understood more of Eric's love for his life's work. She, herself, now became totally absorbed in this Aerial photography.

Just after one P.M. they all mutually agreed on a lunch break. Dan and Violet had already prepared a variety of MRE's which the now, no breakfast, very hungry researches devoured with gusto.

Carlos spoke of his fascination with what the book contained.

" True, they were not able to decode much yet, but

this being just one of hundreds of such books they realized this was really a plethora of advanced knowledge. We are looking at many years of study by our ancestors. From the looks of it, it will also take us many years of study and decoding to sort this all out to understand it."

Mateo spoke at this point.

"This scroll we are looking at is as confusing to us you say the book is. We have identified a few symbols but not in connection with anything we are familiar with. Some of which we have identified appear to be in connection with our counting system and both Venus and the Sun. But at this point we cannot pin anything down to a specific thing. As you indicated it will take many people many months to even get to a basic start. Let's face it, it took our ancestors and others hundreds of years to record and test this theory, if you will. So we cannot expect to do this overnight. Diego was right. We must recruit many people to help, but they must be serious achieve what we want. There are too many doubters in today's world who could undermine all our efforts to date. This study must be kept quiet.

No disagreed. Lunch continued quietly until Eric garnered the attention of all

"I do agree with all that has been discussed so far. I would like to add another suggestion. This is only one book and one scroll. I think we should spend whatever time is necessary at the library to determine if there is an order to these books and scrolls. I suspect there is. To me it is only logical that a people this advanced would not haphazardly put this on a shelf and walk away. If they were out to teach others there would have to be order to their knowledge. So, I suggest we spend what ever time necessary to determine that order. I think that would help greatly in our further studies."

Everyone was now smiling. Carlos stated;

"Who could disagree with that kind of logic. We should continue to work in pairs though. You know, safety in numbers, that sort of thing."

"And we always can rely on our thought transference." added Mario.

Mateo then suggested and all agreed with;

"The pair should be different every day but alternating only one person at a time to maintain a continuity of work. For instance start with Eric and Violet. After a day or so, Carlos and Violet, then Carlos and Mario and so on. With any luck we will all then have an equal knowledge of the library. That could only benefit our studies. Who knows, we may even learn something. With seven of us that should cover a good period of time."

Just as Mateo finished two Howler monkey's let go with their laughing cries.

Diego instantly quipped,

"We now have official approval."

They all laughed and agreed. There plans were accepted. Dan then commented.

"This place is getting to be just as bad as the desert with Mr. Blue."

The rest of the day was a little more easy going. Eric had his chance to study the book more with Carlos. The others continued to share everything they had uncovered.

Violet was now giving a few lessons in the viewing of the air photos to the others.

Diego and Dan along with Mateo continued the work of making the Stelae disappear yet maintaining entrance availability.

Chapter 18

Just after breakfast Colonel Ramirez with three other uniformed men were at the archway. As he approached our table he was his usual formal and proper self. He expressed greetings to us all and a respectful bow to our Queen.

"My friends I think I have finally found a way to be of more help in your endeavors."

He indicated for one of his men to step forward.

"Let me introduce you to one of my treasured sargents. This is Sgt. Benito Cavaliere, a loyal and faithful guardian of our treasured history. He has agreed, at my request, to take a vacation leave from our patrol missions. He can and will be of great assistance in your studies if you will agree to have him join you. He is most knowledgeable in our ancient history which you may count on his sharing. As you already know, serving with me he is well aware of the possible hardships of the jungle. He shall not be a burden to you. I will leave him here with you for now, I must continue my patrol. I will return this evening for your acceptance or not. This way you all may get acquainted. Via con Dios."

With that he turned and headed for the archway before any further discussion could take place.

We all sat there, with I'm sure, dumb looks on our faces. There was a long pause of silence.

Our new member, now smiling, spoke out.

"Let me introduce myself properly."

He spoke with a very slight accent.

"As my Colonel has already told you my name is Benito Cavaliere. I was born and raised not far from here in a small settlement which has since disappeared. My early years of schooling were by my Maya countrymen which is why I still maintain my language skills."

At this point we were all mesmerized by his grasp of the English language, or shall we say the American version of it. By now we were all more relaxed including our new guest.

"Before I continue may I have some of that coffee that is tantalizing my sense of smell?"

Smiles again showed all around as Violet was the first to respond.

"You may not like it the way we do, but give it a try."

Our guest took a long smell and then took a taste. His eyes closed and he smiled a genuine smile.

"It has been a long time since I had a real cup of coffee like this. I may just stay here for the coffee."

With a statement like that he had already won us over.

"Let me go on to sell myself to you. Don't let this uniform and my present position in life betray me. I chose to do what I do. I have studied enough of my native history to know that it needs protection and I want to protect it."

Here he paused almost embarrassed.

"I'm sorry for my outburst. Let me continue my introduction. My very early years of study were at Mexico City university in Maya studies of the Yucatan. My later years of study include a bachelors degree in Archeology from Penn State University. I obtained my Masters in Anthropology slash Archaeology at Harvard University. After Harvard I was fortunate enough to find a backer who financed my trip to Germany where I spent many months studying the translations of the Dresden Codex, which in my opinion belongs back home here from where it was stolen."

He paused here again sipping our black syrup with obvious relish.

Carlos took this opportunity tom ask the obvious.

"With a background like yours why are you stomping around the jungle with a gun?"

Benito smiled at the question.

"I knew you would get around to that. There are so many doubters today that it is hard to get anyone in authority to listen to one dumb native. This group here is the first I have ever come across to do actual real investigative research into my history. I'm sorry I said my, what I really mean is Mayan History. We, and I say this proudly, have always been, in my opinion, one step ahead of the world."

A slight pause,

"I think I'm finished now. I apologize for being so long winded."

He shyly took a seat at the table and sipped some more black liquid with much enjoyment.

"Well, you're one up on us Benito. None of us in all our years of research have ever seen the Dresden Codex. Not only that but very little has been published as to it's contents."

Mario spoke almost with sadness.

"Well, as I stated, is there any way I can be of assistance. It will only be for thirty days and then I will return to my job with the Colonel. He seems to think I can add to your knowledge. I realize that four of you are Mayan and the other three are American., and I know of the heritage of our Queen Lady. Not only native American but of Egyptian heritage. My people go back a long way to that Egyptian connection."

"I see you did your homework." remarked Carlos.

Benito gave a relaxed smile as he answered.

"I try to keep abreast of those who are researching my country and the reasons behind it. We have already lost too much of our treasured history."

Carlos gestured saying, "I can tell by the looks of my colleagues that you are in even if only for thirty days. But," he emphasized the but, "We cannot pay you much."

"Senor` ! I am not here for dollars. I am here to learn

of and preserve my history. My Colonel is still paying me for my vacation time. If all I wanted was dollars I could get a teaching position at a university. I am not here to teach but to learn and preserve my history."

Mario stood and moved to the new guest with his hand extended.

"Senor` Cavaliere, welcome."

This was immediately followed by all. Violet was last and as she approached, he, like the Colonel bowed with the greatest respect.

Diego, in one of his playful moods and with a smile of course remarked, "Anyone who likes coffee the way we drink it has got to be crazy to join us. By the way do you know how to keep the Howler monkey's from being our alarm clocks as early as they do?"

Benito laughed with the rest.

Carlos left the table almost unseen. He went straight for the King's tomb. Eric had a hunch that he went for the new book they put away for safekeeping overnight. Within ten minutes he returned and with the book. The group was still casually chatting about nothing specific. Carlos approached quietly and when close enough he held the book out to this newest member.

"Take a look at this and tell us what you think."

Benito accepted the book and instantly his eyes lit up with excitement. He handled it like a new born slowly opening the cover. He, with super care turned the first few pages. His voice now as excited as his actions asked,

"Where did you get this?"

Carlos, playing dumb answered with a question of his own.

"Why? Is it special?"

Benito, still all smiles answered quickly.

"Why yes. I already recognized items on these first few pages. I saw similar writing in the Dresden Codex."

Excitement showed in everyone now.

Benito continued; "Over the years I have heard rumors about buried hideaways that contained the writings of old.

Like the Dresden Codex but were never found. A lot of the early research and findings are supposedly written in these books. The effects and results of our Astronomy along with other far advanced teachings we inherited from the ever elusive Atlanteans. The people no one believes in that were very real."

"We are some of those who do believe," stated Mateo to Benito's smile as he excitedly continued.

"This book, if it is what I think it is, will unfold and explain our callander system and other extremely important Solar and Lunar movements. Information that we today are only touching on since our travel into outer space. Even these technologies will most likely be rebuffed by some of today's, quote, experts. No one wants to believe there was intelligence before today's modern man."

Here he stopped and with apologetic eyes said, "I'm sorry. I do tend to get carried away sometimes. Forgive me please."

Mario was the first to reply.

"You were only echoing what we all have been saying for many years, which is why we are here doing what we are doing. One other note to really make your day."

Here Mario paused looking at the others. One by one he received a positive nod.

"That book you are holding is only one of possibly a hundred or more."

"You mean !" He hesitated momentarily, "You mean you found the hidden burial place of this ancient knowledge ?"

"We think so," Answered Eric. "But just one of them. We will continue to search for others."

"This is an answer to my prayers." he spouted out like a child on his birthday. Having finally calmed himself Benito asked the obvious.

"Have you decoded any of it yet?"

Eric answered slowly. No not really. We just found this yesterday. We know it will take many people, many months to even get a start on it. Perhaps you would like to help along those lines?"

"I am completely at your service," he answered with a huge smile. "And I will do this willingly for more of that wonderful coffee."

All more relaxed now they went on to tell of their findings to date.

"Did you come across any tunnels yet?"

Diego almost laughed too hard to get the words out.

"We have more tunnels than the New York City subway system. Why do you ask?"

"Over the years I have collected rumors about hidden tunnels that most people laughingly dismiss. But I believe they did exist. Hints from the Atlantean teachers referenced them. How they were built is still a mystery. Perhaps in the translations of these books we may find an answer."

The ever practical Carlos finally put an end to the fun.

"Okay folks, our time is limited as you know so let us continue our planned work. Eric, you and Dove of Spring head back to the library. Benito can come with Mario and me to check out our city limits that we have uncovered to date. The others know their assignments."

The work day started.

~ ~ ~ ~ ~ ~

Eric and Violet took their time walking to the secret entrance in the stelae. Eric reminded Violet that there was still about two hours walk to the library.

"You know we don't have to do this today. We can put it off if you would prefer."

"No, this is fine my love. I would really like to see this treasure trove of books. I must admit though, I am totally fascinated with your Aerial images. I understand why you love it so much. There is a whole world of the unknown in those pictures."

"I'm pleased and proud that you caught on so quickly. Not many do."

At their destination Eric circled the stelae checking its safety.

"I'll feel a lot better when Diego and Dan make this

disappear again.

"They are working on it." comforted Violet.

They quietly entered and opened the access door to the hidden tunnel.

"Now for a relaxing two hour walk," Eric voiced. "We certainly are not wanting for exercise here in the Yucatan. It's far better than the classroom."

After descending the steps they began their two hour walk paying attention to the ever magic lighting that led their way.

"I wonder if you ever get these books deciphered if we will learn the secret of this forever light," remarked Dove of Spring.

"That would be great. The world could use a low cost electric system."

They walked not saying much for forty five minutes or so, then Violet broke their mutual silence

"Eric, have you been paying attention to these walls?"

"Not really, why?"

"Well ----, most are like the other tunnels except for the last twenty feet or so."

"What do you mean? Have they changed?"

"Well! Yes, ever so slightly."

"This magic eyesight of yours. Is it Egyptian, Mayan or Navajo ?"

She smiled at his comment.

"Probably Navajo. You know looking out for the big bad cowboys all the time will sharpen anybody's eyes," she laughed in answer. "Seriously though, there is a difference all of a sudden. They seem smoother as if they were worked by hand more."

She finally stopped, looking to her left she pointed.

"Look come see this."

Eric moved closer to her and to where she was pointing. There was a round indent about the size of his fist.

"Probably an erroneous chip that they smoothed out,"

he offered.

"**I** don't think so," she answered moving closer to the wall yet away from where Eric was standing.

"**L**ook" as she pointed again. "This is exactly the same indent and smoothed out."

The two areas in question were about three and one half feet apart. Without saying anything further Violet was now closely examining the wall, yet only in a certain spot roughly just under three feet away again but off set from a straight line.

"**J**ust as I suspected." she mumbled.

"Suspected what?" quizzed Eric.

"**O**rion again! " she smiled.

"See, two in line and one off set."

"**T**hat's probably just coincidence. You can't put three fingers in these indents. They are too far apart."

Here Violet had a wide smile.

"**B**ut two people could put their hands on them at the same time," she suggested.

"**O**h don't be ridiculous. Why would they design this different from all the others."

"**H**umor me," she answered excitedly.

*"**O**h well, I might as well get this over with so we can continue to the library,"* he thought to himself.

He moved closer to the wall and with out stretched arm placed a fist in two of the curved indents.

Smiling at Eric, violet put her fist in the offset indent.

Nothing.

Eric smiled to himself and was about his hands when an all too familiar sound touched his ears. A small section of wall between he and Violet pivoted open. It was only perhaps two and a half feet wide yet enough for a [person to fit through. The delight showed instantly in Violet's eyes then they suddenly glazed over.

Eric could see she was no longer in this world.

"You have found the way home, my child. I knew you would. It was in your destiny. Do not follow it now.

You have other important matters to fulfill first. Matters for the fulfillment of mankind. A fulfillment he is not aware he needs. Stay by your man. The two of you will redeem your destinies together for the betterment of mankind. I must go now my child. We will talk again when the time is right."

Violet remained in her trance like state for a while as the voice faded. Many seconds later she turned to Eric, smiled and kissed him.

"I love you." she uttered.

Then like a slap in the face she was herself again, but excitedly so.

"She spoke to me again Eric, Nefertiti spoke to me again."

Eric was of course happy for her because he had felt the same elation when ever he conversed with the King.

The two stood there at the entrance to the new tunnel almost not knowing what to do. Eric, being as gentle as possible asked.

"What did the Queen have to say, if I might ask?"

Violet, now back to normal, told Eric of Nefeftiti's words and followed with her own thoughts.

"I wonder what she meant by, You have found the way home?"

Eric was also thinking of that phrase. A slow nagging thought kept trying at Eric, which he purposely kept pushing away. He finally gave in and allowed it to grow.

"Could this mean this is just another worm hole back to Egypt? If so, why? More importantly, how did this come about in the first place. With today's so called advanced science and technology we are only thinking about this existence and even that is only in outer space. Now, suddenly, we have working models of thousands of years ago."

Eric felt a light touch on his arm and realized it was Violet.

"Come back to me Eric. I need you."

He answered with her own words, "I need you."

Sort of normal again he outlined his thoughts to her. She was as excited and confused as he. Smiling a happy face she took a positive lead.

"Let's close this portal and go on to the library. That should be first and foremost to the others."

I had to admit she was absolutely correct. Now we both looked a bit confused. How do we close the wall. We stepped away to study the wall, and as we did it closed automatically. Talk about technology.

They stood back a little to study that wall section. They could find no seams.

"We can look more closely another time. Let's go to the library and check out some books."

He said that with a laugh as if they were back in civilization.

An hour or so of relaxed walking and they reached their goal. Violet was astounded with what she was seeing. This was a resource far larger than the King's tomb. Without any words Violet went right to the scrolls while Eric was drawn again to the books. Trying to think in an orderly manner he reached for a shelf and started in the upper left corner. And carefully extracted the first book. There were no visible marks on the cover, either side. The thin binding gave no hint either.

He laughed to himself as he said, "Why make it easy."

He carefully turned the front cover and viewed it closely. He saw nothing outstanding though there was some markings that he could not read. He truly studied the inside cover in detail but was not satisfied with anything outstanding. Clearing his head as best as possible he glanced at the first page. To him it was all gibberish. This job was really for his Maya friends he decided. The back cover also left him clueless. Setting the first book aside he took down the second in line and studied it the exact same way as the first. Still nothing registered.

"Keep going," he told himself. "It is to easy to give up."

The same routine with numbers three and four. Still nothing. Right now he had four books neatly stacked on the table to his left side.

As he reached for book number five a mark on the pages of the stacked books caught his eye. There, very faint was a design. There was one on each of the four books and all were different.

He called to Violet.

"Please come and look at this."

She put down the scroll she was holding and joined him. Before he could say anything she happily congratulated him.

"You found their number system. I'm proud of you."

Eric looked at her not understanding her words.

"What number system?"

Surprised at his remark she pointed to the first design on the page ends.

"Those numbers would equate to our twentys"

Embarrassed now he asked,

"How do you know?"

"Oh, Carlos showed me some basics of there counting system of old. I remember the symbols, that's all."

"That's all she says. I'm beginning to feel more stupid every day. I guess that's why I need you with me all the time."

She laughed at his remark and kissed him.

"Now can I go back to work sir?"

"No, I need you for a few more minutes."

He retrieved the next few books and showed them to Dove of Spring.

"You're right they are the next two in the number system," She smiled.

"Now I will get back to my scrolls." as she turned and strolled away.

Eric sat there and mumbled to himself. *"No wonder I love that woman."*

Violet was immediately immersed in the scrolls again. She could not actually read them but there were enough familiar symbols that she could tell they also were in an orderly manner.

They tallied for another hour and decided to call it quits. Neither could do the translations which left not much else to do. They still had the two hour trip back to camp. Both were anxious to know what secrets the books held yet also knew they would have to be patient.

On the return trip they paused again at the new tunnel entrance. They spent a little time again looking for seams or hints of the opening. Unfortunately they again came up with zero. They continued their trip home.

Finally returning to the stelae entrance they met Diego and Dan. They, of course had been working on their disappearing magic of the underbrush.

The four headed back to home base looking forward to food and a relaxing evening. They arrived the same time as Colonel Ramirez. The colonel did not stay long once he knew that Benito was welcome for the month. A month if the rains held off.

That night all went through the usual debriefing. Eric and Violet relayed what little they discovered at the library. The fact that there appeared to be a number system on the books was a welcome bit of information. No real progress on the scrolls. The Mayan Glyph's and writing were beyond Violet's capability.

Eric humbly credited Violet with identifying the number system which, of course, led to pick on Eric again.

On the serious side they told of the discovery of yet another tunnel. Benito was ever curious about this. They explained their reasoning for not following it. Eric even hinted that it might be another worm hole. But that would have to be proved at a later time.

The music of the night started somewhat muted but enough to remind everyone that rest was necessary.

~ ~ ~ ~ ~ ~

The Howler Monkey's, ever so true to their job, had everyone up early with louder than normal screeches. This could only mean a large cat was passing through the area. Rifles were at the ready just in case. Benito and Mateo stood watch while coffee and breakfast was prepared. Dan and Eric traded places when they finished eating.

Benito headed for the coffee before the food.

"**I** think I will quit my job just to have this coffee everyday," he punned.

"**T**hen who would help the Colonel protect us without you?" joked back Mario.

The day was planned with Carlos, Mario and Benito taking the library shift. It was agreed that this was the logical choice to start with the translations.

Eric and Violet would research the new tunnel possibilities. This left Mateo with camp duty which satisfied him. He wanted to work on some translations himself of the new book.

The big cat scare seemed to have dissipated. The jungle sounds were normal once more.

The five headed for the stelae. Once there Eric and Violet parted company and pressed on to the tunnel destination. When finally alone they sought out the door markings and almost passed them by. Once recognized again they preformed a thorough search for seams or any sign of definitive markings.

Resigning themselves to no luck they opened the portal and this time, without hesitation, they entered. They were no more than three feet inside when the pivot door closed. At the closing, the forever light showed this entirely new underworld.. Without a word to each other they started a close scan of this side of the portal. This also netted zero results. They could not even find markings to reopen the door.

"**T**hat leaves us with only one choice, forge on ahead," Eric stated firmly.

Violet did not disagree.

They did this willingly and with smiles of curiosity.

Violet took note of Eric's sudden turn to serious. She could hear him mumbling to himself but could not detect the actual words. She let him be rather than spoil his concentration. This self indulgence of his went on for about ten minutes when he finally blurted out,

"Back to the King's tomb."

Violet was naturally startled a bit by this sudden outburst. She in a more quiet voice asked,

"How do you know?"

He stopped and turning to her with a smile of apology explaining.

"Well, we entered this tunnel just about ninety degrees to the other one, and in the shout walk that we have done so far we are constantly turning to the left. The turn is barely noticeable, nevertheless we are turning."

Violet smiled as she answered.

"So that's what all your mumbling was about. You were arguing with yourself again."

He grinned in return.

"Sorry."

Dove of Spring then added,

"So I guess then you also noted that we have been on a slight upward incline."

"I guess I was paying too much attention to notice, but now that you mention it, it makes sense. I'm pretty sure my guess is correct, that we are headed back to the King's tomb."

"Which means..." Violet quickly spoke, "There is possibly another entrance to the tunnel that has yet to be discovered."

"That's is exactly my thinking," Eric answered.

"I thought Carlos and Mario spent a whole day searching again but found nothing."

"Well we will just have to search some more.

Violet with a big smile added,

"Well, what are we waiting for, lead on oh "Chosen One"

Now, hand in hand they moved forward. Violet with her ever alert eyes let no wall detail escape her view. A few times she even caused a halt to further study a section of wall.

"Isn't this forever light a wonderful thing. We must find the secret of this and introduce it to the world."

They continued on slowly, Violet with eyes on the walls while Eric was forever counting steps. He was proud of himself for a change for remembering to bring his small note book and pencil to record his findings. A little more than a hour passed when they came to a dead end. Now it was seam searching time again. The next ten minutes passed without a word. The quiet was only broken by the soft scratching of feet and hands moving against the smooth walls and floor. Neither Eric or Violet located a seam or bump or any questionable area.

Disappointed and disillusioned at this point they sat down resting with backs against the wall. Eric actually closed his eyes to think without distraction. Dove of Spring stretched out in a prone position, her head resting on Eric's thigh staring at nothing. Or was it nothing? She blinked her eyes a few times and even rubbed them slightly. She refocused on the overhead. At first she thought she was so absorbed with Orion Complex that she was seeing things. She closed her eyes for a bit. Upon opening them Orion was still there. It was faint but definitely the three star alignment.

"Eric," she spoke ever so slowly, "You can stop suffering with your thinking now."

He gazed down as he had a slight smile.

Playing a little game now she asked,

"Where do you find stars at night?"

"Now who's being silly?" he answered. "It's time you had a vacation."

Then it suddenly dawned on him and he raised his head and looked up. It was faint yet he too saw Orion. They were both instantly on their feet. Again it took Eric with outstretched arms to touch two stars while Violet, on tiptoe hit the third. Instantly they heard the all too familiar sound. Only this time the ceiling was moving at an angle. They quickly moved to one side and watched the slow motion of the roof reveal steps. Wooden steps. When the movement stopped Eric was at and up the steps. He counted an even dozen but spaced higher than normal household steps.

"After you." Violet said politely as she moved away. Eric took the steps slowly just to be on the safe side. Once he reached the top or at least where he could stand straight up he realized the top was constructed of wood. He slowly reached up with one hand and pushed. It did not budge. He went up one more step and used both arms to push. There was absolutely no movement. He tried one more step and with his back and shoulders and both arms pushed again. He finally quit to ease his back. Nothing had budged. His mind was instantly at work and he moved down a few steps to stretch and relax his muscles. His eyes went to work right away scanning the ceiling that would not move. He finally even gave that up.

"Okay, eagle eye, you try. Not to move it but to find a seam or hinge or whatever."

He stepped aside to let her pass. He finally moved all the way down and sat down, his back against a wall.

Violet was there for a good fifteen minutes before she finally joined Eric on the floor.

"Nothing," she let out slowly with disappointed look

"We will get it," she spoke encouragingly.

They were quiet for a while.

"I wish a compass or GPS would work down underground but there is just too much magnetic disturbance."

"What good would that do?" quizzed Violet.

"To track this tunnel above ground and see what is above us at this point. We will have to do it the hard way. Do you still have the note book?"

She smiled yes.

"Good, because as we leave here I will be counting steps and gauging directions. Hopefully we can duplicate this topside and find out where this leads."

A few minutes later Eric gave one more push upwards. Still no luck.

"Okay, home we go. Get out the notebook madam secretary."

Off they went, Eric counting and Violet recording.

Not much was said on the way back to the stelae except the number of steps and direction that were being recorded. Once back at the starting point they relaxed for a few minutes.

Eric decided to ignore the library trio. They should not be interrupted at all. He hoped they were making progress with Benito's help.

After some fresh air above ground Eric and Violet began their trip back by using what they just recorded in reverse.

Eric's hopes were high that he would now get some answers about this new tunnel. He had his own ideas but now needed physical proof of his own theory. Violet knew how serious he was about this so she remained silent. For now anyway.

The closer they came to camp the more relaxed Eric became. Violet even noticed a smile every now and then. This, of course, made her smile also. Soon she would be able to talk to him again.

They finally came to an area of the jungle that showed obvious signs of digging. Not too recent but the signs were there

Speaking to no one in particular Eric said aloud,

"I knew it. I had a feeling I was right."

"Right about what?" Violet asked softly.

Eric turned to her and quickly apologized.

"I'm sorry my Love. I guess I was locked up in my own world again. To answer your question, this area, now in question, we had done some test digging a couple of years ago with no results. The main places of interest which we can still see were basically cave ins and previously filled in. But if you look at the alignment we had been following, it points to the King's pyramid. Not only that but that is the side of the treasure room. I'm willing to wager that the ceiling we could not open is in the treasure room."

"Are we going there now?" she asked.

"Not just yet. Let's finish our recorded walk. So far it should prove me correct."

"Lead on." she smiled. "At least you're talking to me again," she laughed.

"I'm sorry." he replied sincerely.

They resumed their counted steps and directions. Within a few minutes there was the pyramid in all its splendor.

"It sure is an impressive structure," said Violet to really no one.

Diego was the first to notice their return.

"Any luck with the tunnel hunt?"

"Yes and no," was Eric's non answer. Turning to Violet he asked, "Do we have any more steps left?"

Yes, fifteen to be exact."

"And that will put us well into the pyramid."

"And the treasure room," she added. "Do we go there now?"

"No, we will wait for the others. Besides I think we both deserve a rest."

This brought a big smile to Dove of Spring's lips. She immediately headed for the coffee pot and seated herself at the table. Eric quickly joined her.

~~~~~~

By late afternoon all were gathered at the table for the usual debriefing. Both Eric and Violet could see Carlos was very excited, as were Mario and Benito. So he held off so that the library group could speak. Carlos, without being asked kicked it off.

"Today I think was our most successful in all our years here. The library is probably the most enlightening resource we have found yet. These innumerable books and scrolls will set science on its ear."

"If they accept and believe it." Mario threw in.

"Thanks to our new friend here," he indicated Benito, "We are able to read more than before. We were reviewing a section on Venus today. We knew it was special to our ancestors but we did not know how special. The super accuracy of their callander is actually based on their observations of Venus over countless years, eons even. They performed this feat with out today's telescopes and rocket ships in space. Pure dedication and constant study. Today's
~~~~~~

science could learn from them. Don't get me wrong. I am not knocking their dedication but it could go further. What little we learn today is just a tease. With all these books and scrolls now available we will be able to move forward again."

While Carlos paused Mario jumped right in.

"Don't misunderstand what we are saying. We are still looking at many months if not years, before we will decipher all that is now available to us. Prior to this, we had considered ourselves lucky to have discovered this city. This city as large as it is. Wee can all take pride in this. We all contributed in our own way. But now our work really begins. Less jungle trekking and more study and translations."

Mateo, who was not at the library today, managed to speak.

"Now, perhaps the world will take notice and listen to us. Not just finding this lost city either. About finally proving that some of today's history is completely wrong and will have to be rewritten. Gentlemen and lady, the world before us is now ours. Let us not throw it away."

Diego jumped in at this point.

"You have looked to me for security devices. But this is now bigger than my meager talents. This library and tunnel system must be protected and protected beyond my talents. This must be considered of the utmost importance. Right now even more important than the translations."

All eyes questioned each other now.

On the practical side, no one could disagree with Diego.

Carlos took control again.

"Okay. Tomorrow we will seriously discuss Diego's thoughts before any more translations are undertaken. On this matter I'm sure Benito can also help."

There was a lull and Violet took advantage of the moment.

"Gentlemen, I suggest dinner would be desired at this point. Please continue with your discussion and I will do my best to prepare a celebratory meal for us all."

No one objected.

"While I am doing my wifely duty to my seven husbands Eric can fill you in on our tunnel searching day."

Carlos was the first to immediately comment.

"My dear lady, you are not here to serve us. You are one of us and our equal."

Smiling in answer Violet offered,

"I am well aware of that Carlos and I feel that also, but making dinner for all of is something I want to do right now. I do not feel any less than any of you. Please permit me to pamper you. My pride is now soaring because of my triple heritage, Egyptian, Mayan and Navajo. What could be any better than that. Now you continue on with your discussion and I will make dinner and then to make us even you gentlemen will do the cleanup while I sit and relax."

Her smile while saying this was contagious all around. She took her leave and headed for the food supply tent.

Eric was extra proud.

Eric did take the floor at Violet's suggestion. He explained all that they had done this day right up to the point of the Pyramid.

"So now we just have to find the floor opening in the treasure room." said Mario.

"Negative," answered Eric. " I suggest we just ignore that part of the tunnel. In fact, perhaps even sealing it off."

"Why would we want to do that?" Mateo asked.

"Why not?" answered Eric. It would be just one more thing we would have to be concerned with for security reasons. Securing the library should be of the utmost importance right now. Let's face it there is really no need for that to be used right now. We know it exists and where, that should be enough."

No one disagreed with his reasoning.

Light discussion followed on all the topics discussed so far. Everyone was now more relaxed. Then finally came the words all were ready for.

"Dinner is ready !"

Chapter 19

Dove of Spring and Hunter of Stories were up just before sunrise. As a matter of fact they were awake before the Howler Monkeys. They made their way quietly to the kitchen area and had their famous thick black coffee brewing. Making themselves comfortable at the table they munched on a power bar while waiting for the coffee.

They mutually agreed, quite easily at that, to allow the others free reign with the translations. Dan was working quite well with Diego on the jungle disappearance stuff. That left the other four Mayans for the book decipherment. They both agreed that they would just sort of be in the way.

Once settled with their black brew they tossed ideas around as to what they could do that was worth while to this cause of history. Their long silence was not interrupted by their monkey friends.

Eric finally spoke softly as he looked directly into the eyes of his Queen.

"How would you like to take a ling walk?"

Curious about his statement Violet answered with like softness.

"A walk to where?"

Smiling now, knowing he had her interest Eric answered,

"To Egypt."

His expected reaction was correct. Violet's eyes lit up like fire works.

"When do we start?"

"Well not quite yet. We have to wait for the others first. Who knows they may have other plans for us. This Mayan project is, of course, our first priority."

Her smile dimmed somewhat but not completely. While still alone Violet further questioned.

"When you say walk to Egypt, what do you mean?"

"That crazy worm hole tunnel where we met the guys halfway when we were still in Egypt. Who knows there may be other tunnels off that one. Since you and I appear to be the better tunnel finders, who knows where we could end up. Besides but also important it will give us some much needed alone time."

Smiling softly Violet reached out and touched Eric's hand.

"I miss that very much also. Don't take that the wrong way. I very much like being here, doing what we are doing. But I do miss the us."

No sooner their personal conversation over, the monkey's screeched and one by one the others joined with full coffee mugs. Especially Benito, who smiled heavenly after each welcome sip.

Once all were settled and relaxed, Violet, to the surprise of all, even Eric, started off the days planning.

"Eric and I have been making our own plans, subject of course, to the approval of all of you. It is obvious to all that the study of these new found books and scrolls is first and foremost which sort of leaves us out of active participation. Photographing and recording of these pages is a mountainous job that can not be done in a day or so. That will have to be studied and planned for a more appropriate time with full concentration on only that. I'm sure you all agree on that. In the meantime Eric and I do not want to sit around idol. So we propose to do more tunnel exploration to learn the who, what, when and why of these marvels of construction. The tunnels and the Lost World Parks. We know of three that we saw. We are also sure that there could or will be more. Where? Who knows. The why is also a mystery ti all of us. So this is what we propose. You all continue with your study of these most valuable books. Eric and I will do our tunnel searches in hope of adding to our knowledge of all we are here for. All these things must fit together some how. There has to be a reason for these Lost World Parks, as we refer to them yet none of us has a clue."

She paused here and smiled.

"So, with your permission, allow us to do what we are both good at."

"Very good at," interrupted Carlos with a grin.

Benito, with a most serious face questioned,

"Then who is going to make this wonderful coffee?"

Dan took the liberty to answer.

"We all know how to make it this way and we will show you also."

Benito just smiled.

Violet asserted herself once more.

"Gentlemen that is our proposal. We hope that will fit in with whatever plans you have for the next few weeks."

As Eric looked around he did not detect any negative faces.

Mario spoke out what appeared to be a consensus.

"Only if you promise not to discover too much. We, as you know, are already overwhelmed. When do you want too start and more importantly where?"

Eric now took over for Dove of Spring.

"We thought we would start in the Lost World Park and move on from there throughly checking all the walls."

"And overheads," added a smiling Violet. "These parks must have a purpose, what with their perfection of beauty yet hidden away."

Carlos actually stood to speak.

"My dear Dove of Spring, our Queen of both the Navajo and Maya, you certainly deserve the title. I believe you could talk the screech out of the monkey's if you had a mind to. These words are not meant as an insult, but are spoken on my part and I'm sure the others, with total respect and love. Respect and love well deserved. Follow right now. If you believe that is the path you should follow right now, then so be it. Both you and Eric have our blessing. We know where your hearts lie and that is all that counts. Your decision is based on logic, We know that and we will support you one hundred percent. You truly are Mayan. We wish you luck and hope you return with more of our history."

Violet was now flush with embarrassment but knew Carlos meant what he said. The others agreed heartily.

Now even Eric was somewhat flushed. With that Violet voluntarily reached for the coffee pot and proceeded to fill all mugs. She was fighting back tears. Eric was also drying his eyes with pride for his Queen.

Silence ruled for a time while everyone sought to rein in their emotions. Even Benito, who did not know Violet well was caught up in the emotional scene.

Violet sought out and clasped Eric's hand tightly not wanting to let go.

Finally gathering strength over an emotional struggle she stood and looking from face to face and thanking each one with her eyes and then verbally as well to all.

"**Y**ou honor me too much. I will try to live up to your expectations. You all mean a lot to me. Thank you from my heart."

"**B**reakfast anyone?" yelled Mateo out loud.

Smiles and agreeable nods all around.

Diego chimed in,

"I'll have three eggs scrambled with ham and home fries."

With that came flying anything anyone could pick up.

"Why me? Did I say something wrong?" He laughed.

With the mood of all apparently back to normal each did their own thing about breakfast. Eric and Violet meandered back to their sleeping area to prepare for the tunnel hunt.

Eric made up a light back pack while Violet rigged up a small fanny pack for some light necessities. They each had a canteen of water. Violet made sure she packed a few power bars for each while Eric put away a couple of MRE's for each. A couple of pocket knives and one eight inch hunting knife were also included. Violet finally remembered a small digital camera she had not used yet. *"Who knows?"* she thought. A light change of clothes and they were all set. It was almost noon.

Violet was anxious to get started while Eric was just double checking his double check.

They said their farewells and started for the archway when Eric yelled back.

"Don't wait up for us. We don't know how long we will be. Hours, days, weeks, who knows?"

~ FINI ~

References

Nefertiti's Face
By: Joyce Tyldesley
Pub: Harvard University Press
The Complete Royal Families of Ancient Egypt
By: Adam Dodson
Pub:Thames & Hudson
Sexual Personae
By: Camille Paglir
Pub: Vintage Books
The World of the Pharaohs
By: Christine Hobson
Pub: Thames & Hudson
Akhenaten
By: Conald B. Redford
Pub: Princeton Univ. Press
Ancient Egypt
By: National Geographic Society
Pub: ^ ^ ^
Ancient Egypt
By: Campbell
Pub: Thames and Hudson
A Brief History of Time
By: Stephen Hawking
Pub: Bantam Press
Stephen Hawking, An Unfettered Mind
By: Kitty Ferguson
Pub: Palgrave / MacMillen
Underworld
By: Graham Hancock
Pub: Three River Press

Also by Author
Kenneth J. Goss

Simple Short Stories
(To tingle the Imagination)

Simple Short Stories II
(To further tingle the imagination)

Simple Short Stories III
(Imagine further)

The Dead Living Mummy *
(An epic story of a lost city that ended with a lost mind)

The Innocent Murder
(The tranquility of an English Manor upset by a sudden death)

The Ancient Ones *
(Another adventure with Eric Dexter of the dead Living Mummy)

Ancient History rediscovered
(Third in the Series with Eric Dexter)

The Librarian Checked Out
(A Murder Mystery)

The Jury is Out
(A sequel murder mystery)

The other Planet Earth
(Travel Between Worlds)

The True Cost of Ignorance and False Judgement
(One man's indomitable strength against a town that would destroy him)

The Lost Civilization *
(The fourth in the Eric Dexter Series)

Squiggy the Squirrel Children's Series
also by Author

No.1 The Garden Mystery
No. 2 Squiggy's Special Christmas
The Great New Land
No. 3 New Friends
No. 4 Squiggy and the Bear
No. 5 Squiggy and the Storm
No. 6 The Next Generation
No. 7 Squiggy's Maine Vacation
No. 8 Another double adventure
No. 9 Squiggy and the Virus
No. 10 Suzette Squirrel
No. 11 Squiggy's New Visitors
No. 12 Squiggy's Adventure in the City
No. 13 Squiggy Learns a Lesson
No. 14 Good bye Squiggy

www.ingramcontent.com/pod-product-compliance
Lightning Source LLC
Chambersburg PA
CBHW020923090626
46218CB00001B/48
9798990335042